A BAD CASE OF STRIPES

DAVID SHANNON

THE BLUE SKY PRESS

An Imprint of Scholastic Inc. • New York

To my wife, Heidi;
and to my friend and teacher,
Philip Hays, a.k.a. "Uncle Legend"

THE BLUE SKY PRESS
Copyright © 1998 by David Shannon
All rights reserved.
No part of this publication may be reproduced or stored
in a retrieval system or transmitted in any form or by any
means, electronic, mechanical, photocopying, recording, or
otherwise, without written permission of the publisher.
For information regarding permission, please write to:
Permissions Department,
The Blue Sky Press, an imprint of Scholastic Inc.,
557 Broadway, New York, New York 10012.
The Blue Sky Press is a registered trademark of Scholastic Inc.
Library of Congress catalog card number: 96-54643
ISBN 0-590-92997-6
20 19 18 17   03 04
Printed in the United States of America   37
Designed by David Shannon and Kathleen Westray

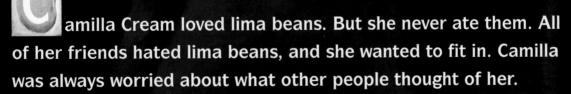

amilla Cream loved lima beans. But she never ate them. All of her friends hated lima beans, and she wanted to fit in. Camilla was always worried about what other people thought of her.

Today she was fretting even more than usual. It was the first day of school, and she couldn't decide what to wear. There were so many people to impress! She tried on forty-two outfits, but none seemed quite right. She put on a pretty red dress and looked in the mirror. Then she screamed.

Her mother ran into the room, and she screamed, too. "Oh my heavens!" she cried. "You're completely covered with stripes!"

This was certainly true. Camilla was striped from head to toe. She looked like a rainbow.

Mrs. Cream felt Camilla's forehead. "Do you feel all right?" she asked.

"I feel fine," Camilla answered, "but just look at me!"

"You get back in bed this instant," her mother ordered. "You're not going to school today."

Camilla was relieved. She didn't want to miss the first day of school, but she was afraid of what the other kids would say. And she had no idea what to wear with those crazy stripes.

That afternoon, Dr. Bumble came to examine Camilla. "Most extraordinary!" he exclaimed. "I've never seen anything like it. Are you having any coughing, sneezing, runny nose, aches, pains, chills, hot flashes, dizziness, drowsiness, shortness of breath, or uncontrollable twitching?"

"No," Camilla told him. "I feel fine."

"Well then," Dr. Bumble said, turning to Mrs. Cream, "I don't see any reason why she shouldn't go to school tomorrow. Here's some ointment that should help clear up those stripes in a few days. If it doesn't, you know where to reach me." And off he went.

The next day was a disaster. Everyone at school laughed at Camilla. They called her "Camilla Crayon" and "Night of the Living Lollipop." She tried her best to act as if everything were normal, but when the class said the Pledge of Allegiance, her stripes turned red, white, and blue, and she broke out in stars!

The other kids thought this was great. One yelled out, "Let's see some purple polka dots!" Sure enough, Camilla turned all purple polka-dotty. Someone else shouted, "Checkerboard!" and a pattern of squares covered her skin. Soon everyone was calling out different shapes and colors, and poor Camilla was changing faster than you can change channels on a T.V.

That night, Mr. Harms, the school principal, called. "I'm sorry, Mrs. Cream," he said. "I'm going to have to ask you to keep Camilla home from school. She's just too much of a distraction, and I've been getting calls from the other parents. They're afraid those stripes may be contagious."

Camilla was so embarrassed. She couldn't believe that two days ago everyone liked her. Now, nobody wanted to be in the same room with her.

Her father tried to make her feel better. "Is there anything I can get you, sweetheart?" he asked.

"No, thank you," sighed Camilla. What she really wanted was a nice plate of lima beans, but she had been laughed at enough for one day.

"Hmm, well, yes, I see," Dr. Bumble mumbled when Mr. Cream phoned the next day. "I think I'd better bring in the Specialists. We'll be right over."

About an hour later, Dr. Bumble arrived with four people in long white coats. He introduced them to the Creams. "This is Dr. Grop, Dr. Sponge, Dr. Cricket, and Dr. Young."

Then the Specialists went to work on Camilla. They squeezed and jabbed, tapped and tested. It was very uncomfortable.

"Well, it's not the mumps," concluded Dr. Grop.

"Or the measles," said Dr. Sponge.

"Definitely not chicken pox," put in Dr. Cricket.

"Or sunburn," said Dr. Young.

"Try these," said the Specialists. They each handed her a bottle filled with different colored pills.

"Take one of each before bed," said Dr. Grop.

Then they filed out the front door, followed by Dr. Bumble.

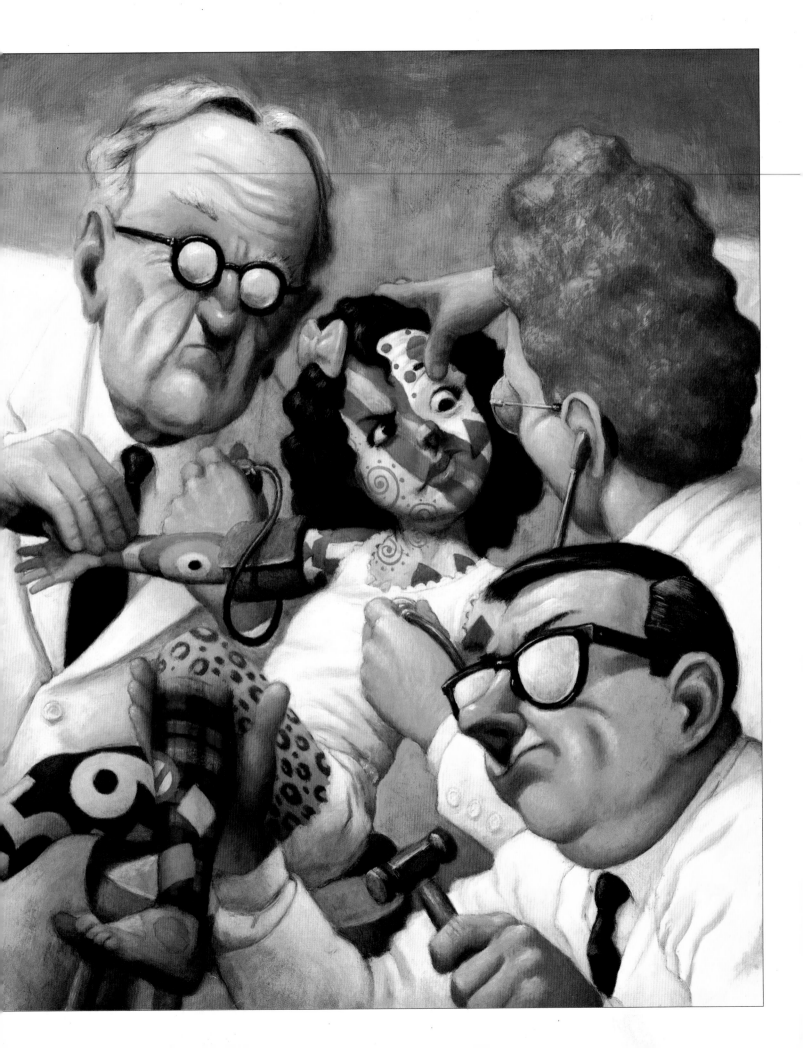

That night, Camilla took her medicine. It was awful. When she woke up the next morning, she did feel different, but when she got dressed, her clothes didn't fit right. She looked in the mirror, and there, staring back at her, was a giant, multi-colored pill with her face on it.

Dr. Bumble rushed over as soon as Mrs. Cream called. But this time, instead of the Specialists, he brought the Experts.

Dr. Gourd and Mr. Mellon were the finest scientific minds in the land. Once again, Camilla was poked and prodded, looked at and listened to. The Experts wrote down lots of numbers. Then they huddled together and whispered.

Dr. Gourd finally spoke. "It might be a virus," he announced with authority. Suddenly, fuzzy little virus balls appeared all over Camilla.

"Or possibly some form of bacteria," said Mr. Mellon. Out popped squiggly little bacteria tails.

"Or it could be a fungus," added Dr. Gourd. Instantly, Camilla was covered with different colored fungus blotches.

The Experts looked at Camilla, then at each other. "We need to go over these numbers again back at the lab," Dr. Gourd explained. "We'll call you when we know something." But the Experts didn't have a clue, much less a cure.

By now, the T.V. news had found out about Camilla. Reporters from every channel were outside her house, telling the story of "The Bizarre Case of the Incredible Changing Kid."

Soon a huge crowd was camped out on the front lawn.

The Creams were swamped with all kinds of remedies from psychologists, allergists, herbalists, nutritionists, psychics, an old medicine man, a guru, and even a veterinarian. Each so-called cure only added to poor Camilla's strange appearance until it was hard to even recognize her. She sprouted roots and berries and crystals and feathers and a long furry tail. But nothing worked.

One day, a woman who called herself an Environmental Therapist claimed she could cure Camilla. "Close your eyes," she said. "Breathe deeply, and become one with your room."

"I wish you hadn't said that," Camilla groaned. Slowly, she started to melt into the walls of her room. Her bed became her mouth, her nose was a dresser, and two paintings were her eyes. The therapist screamed and ran from the house.

"What are we going to do?" cried Mrs. Cream. "It just keeps getting worse and worse!" She began to sob.

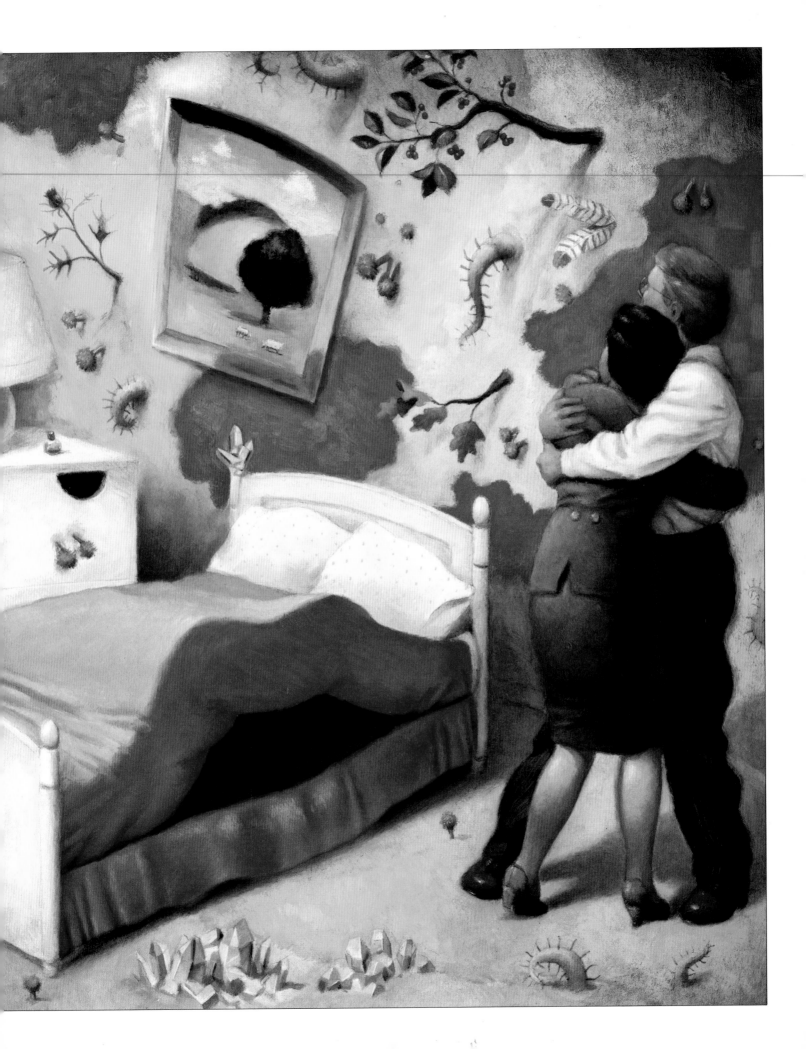

At that moment, Mr. Cream heard a quiet little knock at the front door. He opened it, and there stood an old woman who was just as plump and sweet as a strawberry.

"Excuse me," she said brightly. "But I think I can help."

She went into Camilla's room and looked around. "My goodness," she said with a shake of her head. "What we have here is a *bad* case of stripes. One of the worst I've ever seen!" She pulled a container of small green beans from her bag. "Here," she said. "These might do the trick."

"Are those magic beans?" asked Mrs. Cream.

"Oh my, no," replied the kind old woman. "There's no such thing. These are just plain old lima beans. I'll bet you'd like some, wouldn't you?" she asked Camilla.

Camilla wanted a big, heaping plateful of lima beans more than just about anything, but she was still afraid to admit it.

"Yuck!" she said. "No one likes lima beans, especially me!"

"Oh, dear," the old woman said sadly. "I guess I was wrong about you." She put the beans back in her bag and started toward the door.

Camilla watched the old woman walk away. Those beans would taste *so* good. And being laughed at for eating them was nothing, compared to what she'd been going through. She finally couldn't stand it.

"Wait!" she cried. "The truth is . . . I really love lima beans."

"I thought so," the old woman said with a smile. She took a handful of beans and popped them into Camilla's mouth.

"Mmmm," said Camilla.

Suddenly the branches, feathers, and squiggly tails began to disappear. Then the whole room swirled around. When it stopped, there stood Camilla, and everything was back to normal.

"I'm cured!" she shouted.

"Yes," said the old woman. "I knew the real you was in there somewhere." She patted Camilla on the head. Then she went outside and vanished into the crowd.

Afterward, Camilla wasn't quite the same. Some of the kids at school said she was weird, but she didn't care a bit. She ate all the lima beans she wanted, and she never had even a touch of stripes again.

FOR JEAN CRANE—ALWAYS THERE, ALWAYS FRIEND. —B.J.

TO MOM AND DAD (DLA MAMY I TATY) AND MICHAEL. —R.L.

Patricia Lee Gauch, editor

Text copyright © 2005 by Barbara Joosse. Illustrations copyright © 2005 by Renata Liwska. All rights reserved. This book, or parts thereof, may not be reproduced in any form without permission in writing from the publisher, PHILOMEL BOOKS, a division of Penguin Young Readers Group, 345 Hudson Street, New York, NY 10014. Philomel Books, Reg. U.S. Pat. & Tm. Off. The scanning, uploading and distribution of this book via the Internet or via any other means without the permission of the publisher is illegal and punishable by law. Please purchase only authorized electronic editions, and do not participate in or encourage electronic piracy of copyrighted materials. Your support of the author's rights is appreciated.
Published simultaneously in Canada. Manufactured in China by South China Printing Co. Ltd.
Designed by Semadar Megged. Text set in 15-point Caslon 3.
Library of Congress Cataloging-in-Publication Data   Joosse, Barbara M.
Nikolai, the only bear / by Barbara Joosse; illustrated by Renata Liwska.   p. cm.
Summary: Nikolai, a bear who lives in the orphanage in Novosibirsk, Russia, does not seem to fit in until the day some visitors arrive from America.
[1. Orphans—Fiction. 2. Orphanages—Fiction. 3. Bears—Fiction. 4. Novosibirsk (Russia)—Fiction. 5. Russia—Fiction.] I. Liwska, Renata, ill. II. Title.
PZ7.J7435Ni 2005   [E]—dc22   2004010426
ISBN 0-399-23884-0
1 3 5 7 9 10 8 6 4 2
First Impression

Then the fur-faced man,
the smooth-faced woman—
and Nikolai—
leave for America.

Together,
they go home.

When it's time to go,
the ninety-nine keepers
and ninety-nine orphans wave goodbye.

Nikolai paws the air.

The smooth-faced woman opens her arms in a circle.
Nikolai crawls inside the hug,
where she holds him tight.
In the woman's arms,
Nikolai feels soft-bearish.

After many visits,
the fur-faced man says, "Nikolai, our home is far away,
in America. It's time for us to leave."

"We'd like you to come with us and be part of our family,"
says the smooth-faced woman.
"We'd like you to be our son."

Dr. Larissa interprets the words in Russian,
but Nikolai already understands.

The man prowls with Nikolai on the red, red rug.

The woman sings songs to him.
Her voice makes Nikolai feel soft-bearish.
They make him want to crawl on her lap.

One day, he does.

The visitors come every day.

They attend music class with Nikolai
and watch proudly as he plays with others.

The next day,
there are two visitors—
the fur-faced man and a smooth-faced woman.
The smooth-faced woman has moonlight hair
and lake water eyes.

Nikolai holds up his paws and claws the air.
He waits for the smooth-faced woman to say, "Play nice."
But she does not.

The smooth-faced woman claws the air
and holds Nikolai's paw in hers.

One snowy day,
a visitor arrives at Orphanage Number One,
in Novosibirsk, Russia.
He has a fuzzy head and furry face.
Nikolai has never seen a furry face before,
except on the poster beside his bed.

The visitor crouches down on his hind legs
so his face is even with Nikolai's.
His eyes are soft and brown.

"Hello, Nikolai," says the visitor.

Nikolai growls hello.
The visitor growls back.

Dear Mr. and Mrs. Martin,

Nikolai is a lively three-year-old. He is very healthy. He's not speaking yet, but perhaps he will talk soon. We're trying to teach him to play well with others. I think a loving family will help in these matters.

We believe Nikolai will make a wonderful addition to your family. We look forward to meeting you soon!

Dr. Larissa

Dr. Larissa writes a letter to America.

Many orphans come and go. Nikolai stays.
He has not found a family.

At night,
a babushka zips Nikolai into his pajamas.
He crawls into his own little cave.
The babushka turns off the sun
and lights the moon.

"*Grrrrr,*" says Nikolai.

"Say goodnight, Nikolai," says the babushka,
but Nikolai already did.

Nikolai does sing the words. He sings Bear words,
but Miss Sonya doesn't speak Bear.

Every afternoon,
all the orphans—and Nikolai—go to music class.
Miss Sonya plays the accordion while the orphans sing.
Nikolai bellows.
"Sing the *words*, Nikolai," Miss Sonya says.

Now Nikolai is three years old.

Every morning,
all the orphans—and Nikolai—play together
on the red, red rug.
Nikolai likes to play "chase."
The orphans scream and run away.

"Play nice, Nikolai," says the keeper.

When Nikolai was nine months old, he began to talk.
His first word was "Hello."
He said it like this: *"Rrroaar."*

Nikolai's keeper didn't understand Bear.
"Say 'Good morning,' Nikolai," she said.

NIKOLAI lives at Orphanage Number One
in Novosibirsk, Russia.
There are ninety-nine keepers
and one hundred orphans.

Nikolai is the only bear.

NIKOLAI, THE ONLY BEAR

BARBARA JOOSSE

Illustrated by Renata Liwska

Philomel Books

Like illegal immigration, education remains a major issue for New Mexico. In 2006, the state placed 48th out of the 50 states in education spending. Today, it ranks 20th. Susana Martinez, who took office in 2011 as the first Hispanic woman governor in the United States, supports spending more money on education and passed reforms that included rating each school's performance. New Mexico continues to be rich in oil, natural gas, and other resources that help provide the state with funds for its important programs. As always, it is New Mexico's people—more than 50 percent of whom are members of minority populations—who will keep things moving in the right direction.

Roswell Army Air Field

ANNIE DODGE WAUNEKA: LIFE SAVER

The Navajos, like all Native Americans, have often faced hard times on their reservations. Improving health care was a great need. Annie Dodge Wauneka (1910–1997) played a large part in making sure the Navajos had modern medical care. Born in Arizona, she attended school in Albuquerque. Her father was a Navajo tribal leader, and she often traveled with him in New Mexico to visit Navajo villages. In 1951, she followed her father onto the Navajo Tribal Council, and she made health issues her top concern. She considered tuberculosis—an infection that attacks the lungs—the number-one enemy. By making sure Navajos received medical care, she is thought to have saved the lives of 2,000 people. Her efforts won her the Presidential Medal of Freedom in 1963.

? **Want to know more?** Visit www.factsfornow.scholastic.com and enter the keywords **New Mexico**.

64

READ ABOUT

Shoppers at an
outdoor market
in Santa Fe

PEOPLE

★

NEW MEXICO'S CULTURE HAS BEEN LARGELY SHAPED BY FOUR GROUPS OF PEOPLE: NATIVE AMERICANS, HISPANICS,* AFRICAN AMERICANS, AND WHITE EUROPEANS. Later arrivals from Asia and other parts of the world added to the mix, bringing their own traditions. New Mexico's population is small—it ranks 36th out of the 50 states—but growing. People come for jobs, warm weather, and to enjoy New Mexico's unique mix of cultures.

*For consistency within the America the Beautiful series of books, the editors chose to use the word Hispanics. But in New Mexico, people of Spanish descent refer to themselves as Hispanos.

Crowds at the 2012 New Mexico State Fair in Albuquerque

Big City Life

This list shows the population of New Mexico's biggest cities.

Albuquerque	545,852
Las Cruces	97,618
Rio Rancho	87,521
Santa Fe	67,947
Roswell	48,366

Source: U.S. Census Bureau, 2010 census

CITIES, VILLAGES, NATIONS

Albuquerque, with more than 540,000 people, is the largest city in New Mexico. About one-quarter of the state's population calls the city home, and tens of thousands more live in the surrounding suburbs. As a center for business, arts, and education, Albuquerque buzzes with activity. Yet the city is near many natural wonders and open spaces, so people can easily take a break from city life.

Sizable cities, such as Santa Fe, Las Cruces, Gallup, and Rio Rancho, are scattered around the state. But small towns and villages are more common. Some are nestled high in the mountains. Others consist of nothing more than a few buildings that dot the high desert. Satellite dishes help bring the Internet and television to these remote areas. But many rural residents enjoy being far from the hustle and bustle of city life.

Where New Mexicans Live

The colors on this map indicate population density throughout the state. The darker the color, the more people live there.

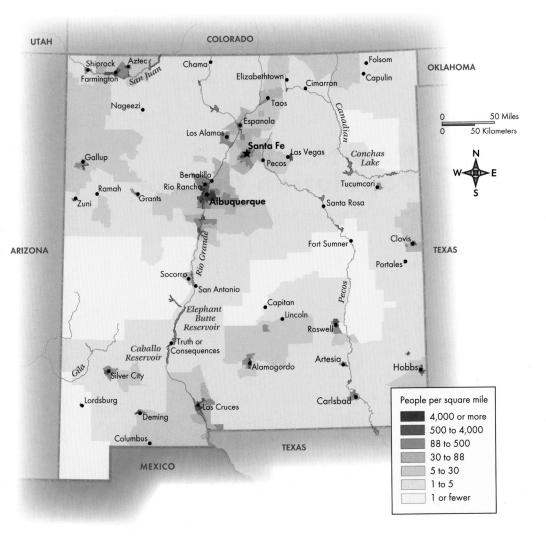

People per square mile

■	4,000 or more
■	500 to 4,000
■	88 to 500
■	30 to 88
■	5 to 30
■	1 to 5
□	1 or fewer

Although New Mexico is a state, it is also home to several dozen "nations." Each Native American pueblo and reservation is considered a nation, with its own leaders and laws. Some Native Americans choose to live outside Native lands and return only for special events. Those who remain on Native lands pursue a variety of lifestyles. Many people live completely modern lives, commuting to and from jobs, and embracing the latest technology. But at the ancient village of Taos Pueblo, some people live as their ancestors did hundreds of years ago. They have no electricity, and they still bake bread in traditional adobe ovens. Other Taos Pueblo people live in modern homes and visit the village to participate in traditional events.

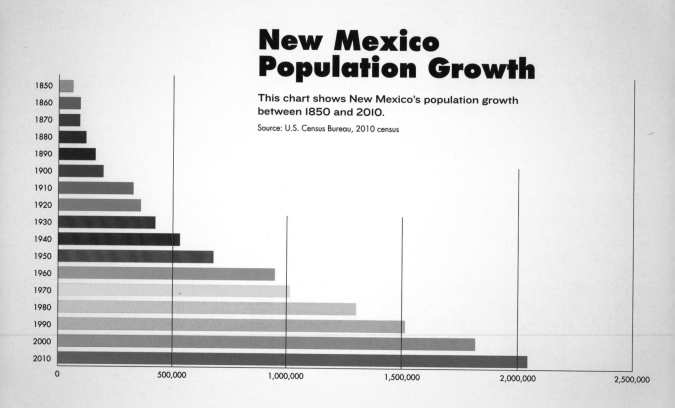

New Mexico Population Growth

This chart shows New Mexico's population growth between 1850 and 2010.

Source: U.S. Census Bureau, 2010 census

This Navajo woman raises sheep, spins their wool, and weaves it into rugs.

THE PEOPLE OF NEW MEXICO

Saying that New Mexico is a mix of Native American, Hispanic, African American, and white cultures doesn't paint a full picture of the state. Within each group, there are distinct differences. The Native Americans include the 19 Pueblo groups, two groups of Apaches, the Navajos, and Native Americans who moved from the Great Plains. Even some of the Pueblo groups are distinct: three different languages are spoken at the pueblos.

The Hispanics of New Mexico include families who trace their roots to the first Spanish settlers, as well as recent arrivals from Mexico and Central America. The state's white population includes people from many

MINI-BIO

N. SCOTT MOMADAY: THE INDIAN EXPERIENCE

N. Scott Momaday (1934–), a Kiowa from Oklahoma, spent much of his youth at Jemez Pueblo. For a time, he also lived on Apache and Navajo reservations. As an adult, he explored his Native American background in words. In 1968, he published his first novel, *House Made of Dawn*. The book won a Pulitzer Prize, a major award for U.S. writers. His other writings include poems, stories, and articles about Native American history. Momaday believes living among Indians from different nations was a good experience: "We didn't have the same language, but I always had a sense of being one of them because I'm Indian. . . . We got along well because we were all Indians together."

? Want to know more? Visit www.factsfornow .scholastic.com and enter the keywords **New Mexico**.

European backgrounds. Some came from the eastern United States. Others came from Ireland, Italy, and eastern Europe. More recently, people have arrived from Germany and Canada. A growing number of Asians are also settling in New Mexico, particularly in Albuquerque and other cities. The African American population has been growing since 1970, now making up 1.7 percent of the state's population. Some can trace their roots to the Buffalo Soldiers or workers who came west to build railroads.

People QuickFacts

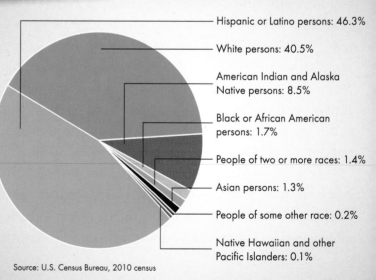

- Hispanic or Latino persons: 46.3%
- White persons: 40.5%
- American Indian and Alaska Native persons: 8.5%
- Black or African American persons: 1.7%
- People of two or more races: 1.4%
- Asian persons: 1.3%
- People of some other race: 0.2%
- Native Hawaiian and other Pacific Islanders: 0.1%

Source: U.S. Census Bureau, 2010 census

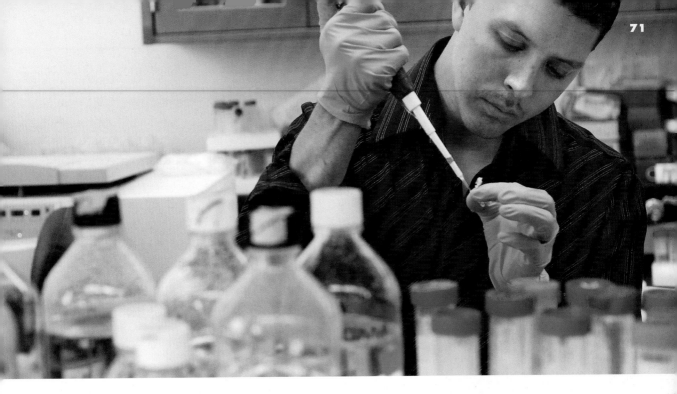

A student works in a laboratory at the University of New Mexico in Albuquerque.

LEARNING FOR LIFE

New Mexicans were slow to build public schools, and for centuries the Catholic Church educated the young. Today, public, private, and religious schools all give students the learning they need to succeed in life. The state is making an extra effort to improve education among Native Americans. This includes teaching students their native language in addition to English.

Students who go on to college have many choices if they stay in the state. The largest school is the University of New Mexico in Albuquerque, with branches in Gallup, Los Alamos, Taos, and Valencia. The school is well known for its work in Latin American history and the history of the American West. Other important state-run schools are New Mexico State University in Las Cruces, the New Mexico Institute of Mining and Technology in Socorro, and Highlands University in Las Vegas. New Mexico also has several small private colleges, including St. John's College in Santa Fe.

HOW TO TALK LIKE A NEW MEXICAN

To talk like a New Mexican, you might want to know a few words of Spanish. Drive through most New Mexican neighborhoods and you're sure to see large red chile peppers tied to a string. That long tail of peppers is called a *ristra*. One term from Caló (Mexican Spanish slang) is *nel, pastel,* which means "no way" (literally "no cake"). But New Mexico has a cowboy heritage, too. Cowboys and cowgirls might call an outspoken person a "maverick," like an unbranded animal. When a rider is thrown from a horse, some say he is "tasting gravel."

HOW TO EAT LIKE A NEW MEXICAN

As with so much in New Mexico, food is inspired by a blend of several cultures. Native American and Mexican cuisine are both popular throughout the state. In addition, immigrants from around the world brought food ranging from egg rolls to pizza.

Perhaps the one food most connected to New Mexico is the chile pepper. Spanish settlers brought the first chiles with them from Mexico. To the rest of the United States, they're "chili" peppers, but you'd better change that last "i" to an "e" in New Mexico. Local residents insist that the traditional Spanish spelling, "chile," be used. Many peppers are green when they're picked, but they turn shades of red as they dry in the sun.

FAQ

Q8 WHAT DOES "RED OR GREEN?" MEAN IN A RESTAURANT?

A8 "Red or green?" is the official state question in New Mexico. It means, "Do you want red chile sauce or green chile sauce with your food?" People who can't decide sometimes answer "Christmas," which means a little bit of both.

Hot chile peppers

MENU

WHAT'S ON THE MENU IN NEW MEXICO?

★ ★ ★

Sopaipilla

The New Mexican sopaipilla is a creation that likely dates back to colonial Albuquerque. A thin square of wheat flour is fried in oil. While it cooks, it puffs up like a small, hollow pillow. Some people put meat, cheese, or peppers inside. Others cover the treat with honey.

Posole

This stew features corn, pork, and chiles, all cooked together for several hours. In southern New Mexico, only red chiles are used, but northerners sometimes use green instead. In any color, posole makes a hearty meal, and it's often a favorite on Christmas Eve.

"Cowboy" Food

Long ago, cowboys cooked potatoes, beans, and meat over open flames while they moved cattle across the plains. Those foods are still part of many New Mexican meals.

Piñon

Piñon pine trees grow in New Mexico's mountains. Their nuts turn up in all sorts of recipes in New Mexico, from breads to candy. Some say the best way to eat these pine nuts is roasted.

TRY THIS RECIPE
Red Chile Sauce

New Mexicans know something about chile peppers—they've grown them for more than 400 years. Here's a recipe for one of New Mexico's favorite foods, a sauce you can use to spice up tacos, enchiladas, and anything else that seems a little bland. Have an adult help you with this recipe.

Ingredients:
10 to 12 dried red chiles
1 medium onion, chopped
2 cloves garlic, chopped
2 tablespoons vegetable oil
1 cup water

Instructions:
1. Split open the chiles and remove the stems and seeds. (Be sure not to touch your eyes after working with the chiles—it will hurt!) Rinse off the chiles and place them in a pot. Cover them with hot water. Let the chiles sit for 15 minutes and then remove them from the water. You can save some of the water to use in step 3.
2. Sauté the onion and garlic in the oil until they are soft, about 5 minutes.
3. Place all the ingredients and the cup of water into a blender or food processor. Mix until you have a fiery red sauce!

Piñon nuts

MINI-BIO

MARIA MARTINEZ: MASTER POTTER

Maria Martinez (1887–1980) made Pueblo pottery a widely admired art form. She was born at San Ildefonso, where she learned pottery from her aunt. Martinez demonstrated her work at the St. Louis World's Fair in 1904. By 1919, she had developed her famous black on black pottery, in which black designs are set on a shiny black background. She also did something other Native American potters had not—she signed her name on her work. Soon her work was winning prizes and commanding high prices. Her husband, Julian, painted the designs on many of her pieces. Together, they taught their style to their children. Members of the Martinez family still make black on black pottery.

 Want to know more? Visit www.factsfornow .scholastic.com and enter the keywords **New Mexico**.

KEEPING TRADITION ALIVE

For centuries, the Pueblo have made pottery, baskets, jewelry, and weavings. The items were meant for daily use, but they were also artistic creations. These skills have been passed down, and Native Americans in New Mexico today continue the artistic traditions.

Each Pueblo has its own style of pottery. At Taos, some potters still shape their work by hand, while Native Americans elsewhere use a turning wheel to help shape their creations.

A jeweler in his workshop at the Santo Domingo Pueblo

Navajo rugs for sale in Santa Fe

MINI-BIO

GEORGE LÓPEZ: A CARVER'S CRAFT

As a boy, George López (1900–1993) watched his father, José, carve santos out of aspen wood. The family lived in Córdova, a small town near the Sangre de Cristo Mountains. Carvers in this remote area had kept alive the craft of wood-carving, which dates back to the 18th century. George (seen here with his wife, Sabinita) became a carver, too. He was well known for his unpainted santos, carrying on the style he learned from his father. Today, other members of the López family continue to work as santeros.

? Want to know more? Visit www.factsfor now.scholastic.com and enter the keywords **New Mexico**.

Some Jemez potters paint animals on their work, and certain potters of San Ildefonso specialize in making black pottery. Collectors pay thousands of dollars for the work of the best Pueblo artists. Weaving is a specialty of the Navajos. Navajo rugs and blankets are prized the world over for their designs, which often feature zigzag lines and geometric shapes. Native Americans in New Mexico also make jewelry. They often work in silver and turquoise.

The Spanish settlers also had their crafts, which have endured. In colonial days, carvers made statues and wooden screens that showed saints or people from the Bible. The general name for these is *santos*—"saints"—and the artists are called *santeros*. Today, New Mexico's santeros carve both religious items and images from everyday life.

MINI-BIO

GEORGIA O'KEEFFE: PAINTER OF THE DESERT

Wisconsin native Georgia O'Keeffe (1887–1986) made her first long visit to New Mexico in 1929 and fell in love with its scenery and light. She returned each summer for several years. Then, in 1940, she bought an adobe house near Abiquiu, west of Taos. She knocked down some of its walls and put in glass, to make it easier to paint her surroundings. She collected animal bones in the desert, which also appeared in her work. Some art historians consider O'Keeffe one of the world's great painters, and her images of New Mexico are among her best works.

 Want to know more? Visit www.factsfor now.scholastic.com and enter the keywords **New Mexico**.

Ernest Blumenschein seated in front of his painting *The Extraordinary Affray* in 1927

MODERN ART

Georgia O'Keeffe an artist known for her paintings of flowers, cattle bones, and landscapes. A well-known Western artist, Ernest Blumenschein, helped make Taos a center for art. He was known for painting the scenery and people he saw around him. Both O'Keeffe and Blumenschein moved to New Mexico from the East. Native-born artists include Peter Hurd, who also painted images of Western scenery, and R. C. Gorman, a Navajo, who won fame for his colorful images of Navajo women. Chiricahua Apache sculptor Allan Houser studied in Santa Fe before becoming famous for his works in wood, bronze, and stone. Sculptor Glenna Goodacre has a studio in Santa Fe. Her work includes the image of the Shoshone guide Sacagawea that is found on U.S. dollar coins.

A MUSICAL LAND

Music has filled the air of New Mexico for several thousand years. The Ancestral Pueblo people used drums and dance in their ceremonies, and so do today's Native people. Tom Bee, originally from Gallup, is perhaps the best-known Indian musician in the state. For more than 30 years, he has written, played, and produced Native American music. At times he blends traditional styles with modern rock and pop. The drum group Black Eagle of Jemez Pueblo formed in 1989. They perform at traditional powwows and won the 2004 Grammy Award for best Native American music album.

Mariachi music, which originated in Mexico, is also popular in New Mexico. Mariachi bands usually include several guitars, violins, and a trumpet. They often play at weddings. Like mariachi music, folk dancing called folklorico traces its roots to Mexico and is popular among the Hispanic residents of New Mexico. The Albuquerque-based Pimentel & Sons Guitar Makers contribute to local and international music with their classical musical instruments crafted completely by hand.

Taos drums

Writer Rudolfo Anaya
at a book signing in
Albuquerque

NEW MEXICAN WRITERS

Tony Hillerman was a popular novelist who wrote detective stories featuring two Navajos as the heroes. Poet and scholar Luci Tapahonso is from Shiprock. She often writes in her native Navajo language. Rudolfo Anaya first won fame with his novel *Bless Me, Ultima*, the story of a Hispanic teen living in a small New Mexico town. He has also

Folk dancers perform at the annual Tularosa Fiesta.

MINI-BIO

JIMMY SANTIAGO BACA: FINDING A VOICE

Born of Hispanic and Apache descent in Santa Fe, Jimmy Santiago Baca (1952–) had a challenging childhood. After his parents abandoned him, he was raised by his grandmother and then sent to an orphanage. Baca ran away at age 13, and by age 21, he was in prison for drug possession. During his time in prison, Baca taught himself to read and write. A fellow inmate encouraged him to send some of his first poems to *Mother Jones* magazine, which printed them. Since then, Baca has become a celebrated poet, novelist, and playwright. In 2004, he established Cedar Tree, a nonprofit organization that helps prisoners and at-risk youths find their voices through writing.

 Want to know more? Visit www.factsfor now.scholastic.com and enter the keywords **New Mexico**.

written several children's books, including *The Farolitos of Christmas*, which describes the New Mexican tradition of lighting *farolitos* (lanterns).

ON THE BALL

New Mexico doesn't have any major professional sports teams, but that doesn't mean folks don't have something to cheer about. Albuquerque is home to a minor league baseball team called the

Isotopes. The Isotopes' home field also hosts the annual Native American All-Star Game, which features players from Pueblo teams.

The University of New Mexico, Albuquerque, has a number of outstanding sports teams, nicknamed The Lobos. Its men's soccer team is usually ranked as one of the best in the country. The women's basketball program is also highly ranked, and the football team has sent several players to the pros. The best-known is New Mexico native Brian Urlacher, one of the top linebackers in the National Football League. New Mexico State also has a successful college sports program.

New Mexicans have played a big part in two sports that couldn't be more different: auto racing and ballooning. The Unser family of Albuquerque has produced several top race-car drivers. Al Unser, brother Bobby, and Al's son Al Jr. have a total of nine wins at the Indianapolis 500, one of the world's most famous races. Traveling at a much slower speed, balloonists compete in Albuquerque's yearly fiesta. Balloonists try to fly the farthest distance, land in certain areas, or race to reach a target before the other balloons. In 1978, New Mexico balloonists Maxie Anderson, Ben Abruzzo, and Larry Newman made the world's first balloon trip across the Atlantic Ocean.

New Mexicans from all walks of life are making their mark. And they know that their state is a great place to call home.

NANCY LOPEZ: GREAT GOLFER

Champion golfer Nancy Lopez (1957–) perfected her game as a young girl in Roswell. At 12, she was the top women's golfer in the state. At Goddard High School in Roswell, she played for the boy's team. Few high schools in the United States had many sports teams for girls at that time. Lopez's precise drives and putts made the team state champions. In 1978, she began playing professionally. During her career, she won 48 tournaments.

? **Want to know more?** Visit www.factsfor now.scholastic.com and enter the keywords **New Mexico**.

READ ABOUT

New Mexicans vote
in a 2012 election.

CHAPTER SEVEN

GOVERNMENT

★

IN 2006, JORDAN MCKITTRICK WAS A 15-YEAR-OLD STUDENT IN SANTA FE. He met two survivors of World War II and developed an interest in ending wars. So he and eight other New Mexicans visited U.S. senator Pete Domenici. The group wanted the senator to seek a quick end to the war in Iraq. Some New Mexicans like Jordan oppose the war. Others support it, and thousands of New Mexicans serve in the military. New Mexicans differ on many issues, and they count on their leaders to balance opposing views when they make decisions for the state.

The state capitol in Santa Fe

THE CENTER OF STATE GOVERNMENT

Santa Fe has served as the capital of New Mexico, first as part of New Spain, then as part of Mexico, and finally as one of the United States. Today, New Mexico lawmakers meet at the state capitol, which is known as the Roundhouse. The governor and lieutenant governor have offices there. The state's supreme court meets in Santa Fe in its own building not far from the Roundhouse. This building opened in 1937.

Capitol Facts

Here are some facts about New Mexico's state capitol.

Number of stories . . . . 3, plus one level belowground
Height . . . . 60 feet (18 m)
Opened 1966
Cost of construction . . . . $4.7 million

Capital City

This map shows places of interest around Santa Fe, New Mexico's capital city.

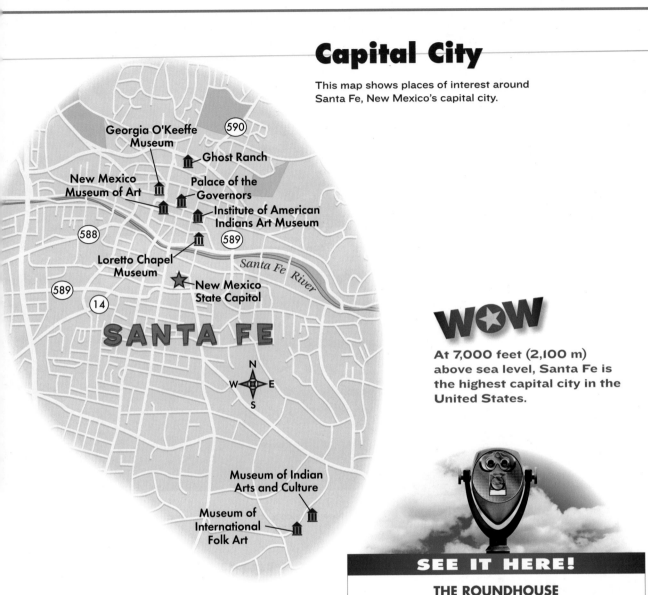

590

Georgia O'Keeffe Museum

Ghost Ranch

New Mexico Museum of Art

Palace of the Governors

Institute of American Indians Art Museum

588

589

Loretto Chapel Museum

New Mexico State Capitol

589

14

SANTA FE

N W E S

Santa Fe River

Museum of Indian Arts and Culture

Museum of International Folk Art

WOW

At 7,000 feet (2,100 m) above sea level, Santa Fe is the highest capital city in the United States.

SEE IT HERE!

THE ROUNDHOUSE

The Roundhouse is the only round capitol in the United States. Built partly in a Pueblo adobe style, the Roundhouse has four short wings jutting out at equal points around the circle. From above, the building looks a little like the Zia Pueblo sun symbol, which is shown on New Mexico's state flag. The Roundhouse is the fourth building in Santa Fe to have served as the capitol of New Mexico. The first capitol building was the historic Palace of the Governors, which is now a museum of New Mexican history.

New Mexico's government, like the federal government, has three branches. The legislative branch makes laws, the executive branch carries out the laws (and often proposes new ones), and the judicial branch makes sure the laws are carried out fairly.

REPRESENTATIVE
han "... Cote
... AN ... 3

REPRESENTATIVE
Mimi S...ewart
D-BERN... 0-21

REPRESENTATIVE
Henry Kiki Saavedra
D-BERNALILLO-10

...ENTATIVE
...golf, Jr.
...NTA FE-47

REPRESENTATIVE
Nick L. Salazar
D-COLFAX, MORA, R.A., S.M.-40

New Mexico's representatives discuss a new law.

Representing New Mexico

This list shows the number of elected officials who represent New Mexico, both on the state and national levels.

OFFICE	NUMBER	LENGTH OF TERM
State senators	42	4 years
State representatives	70	2 years
U.S. senators	2	6 years
U.S. representatives	3	2 years
Presidential electors	5	—

THE LEGISLATIVE BRANCH

New Mexico lawmakers form the state legislature, which includes the house of representatives and the senate. The representatives and senators present bills (proposals for new laws). The bills are debated and then voted on by both the house and the senate. Both parts of the legislature must approve a bill before it is sent to the governor, who decides whether or not the bill will become law.

MINI-BIO

SUSANA MARTINEZ: LEADING THE WAY

Susana Martinez (1959–) was born in El Paso, Texas, to a hardworking middle-class family. After college, Martinez studied law in Oklahoma and then moved to New Mexico, where she became a prosecutor, handling child-abuse and murder cases. When a new district attorney was elected, she was fired, but she soon ran against him, winning the election. Eventually, Martinez served four terms as a district attorney in New Mexico. In 2011, the Republican leader became the first woman governor of New Mexico as well as the country's first female Hispanic governor.

? **Want to know more?** Visit wwwfactsfor nowscholastic.com and enter the keywords **New Mexico**.

The legislature tackles all sorts of problems. Entering the 21st century, New Mexico's students often did not perform as well as students in other states. In response, lawmakers wrote bills that called for taxpayer-funded prekindergarten classes across New Mexico.

Voters also have a say in the lawmaking process. They can try to get rid of a law through a process that is called referendum. After enough people sign a **petition**, voters can decide whether or not the law stays on the law books.

WORD TO KNOW

petition *a list of voters' signatures requesting some action*

86

MINI-BIO

OCTAVIANO LARRAZOLO: POLITICAL LEADER

When New Mexico was a U.S. territory, all but one of its governors were white. After New Mexico became a state, voters chose Octaviano Larrazolo (1859–1930) as their first Hispanic governor in 1918. Larrazolo was born in Mexico, but settled in New Mexico in 1895. He worked as a teacher and a lawyer before entering politics. During the 1920s, he served in the New Mexico state legislature. Then, in 1928, he became the first Hispanic to sit in the U.S. Senate. Illness forced him to leave that post after only a few months.

Want to know more? Visit www.factsfornow.scholastic.com and enter the keywords **New Mexico**.

The New Mexico commissioner of public lands manages some 13 million acres (5 million hectares) of land with valuable natural resources. That's an area about the size of Massachusetts and Vermont combined.

THE EXECUTIVE BRANCH

The governor is one of seven executive branch positions elected by New Mexicans. The governor is the leader of the executive branch and chooses people to lead various departments. The legislature must approve these choices. The governor also signs bills into law and proposes the state budget. The state lawmakers, however, have the final say on how much money is spent and where it goes.

The lieutenant governor of New Mexico steps in to lead the executive branch if the governor is out of the state or otherwise can't serve. Other executive branch offices include secretary of state, attorney general, treasurer, and auditor. The commissioner of public lands watches over the money the state makes from its natural resources. These include oil, natural gas, and minerals. Most of the money earned from these resources goes to the state's schools.

THE JUDICIAL BRANCH

Finding plenty of water is tough for many New Mexico communities. For decades, a town could use as much water as it wanted from local sources, even if that meant there was little water left for other towns. In 2004, however, the state supreme court overturned this rule, which traced its roots back to colonial days.

The state supreme court is just one part of New Mexico's judicial branch. In most cases, voters choose

New Mexico's State Government

EXECUTIVE BRANCH
Carries out state laws

Governor

Lieutenant Governor

Secretary of State

Attorney General

Treasurer

Auditor

LEGISLATIVE BRANCH
Makes and passes state laws

Senate (42 members)

House of Representatives (70 members)

JUDICIAL BRANCH
Enforces state laws

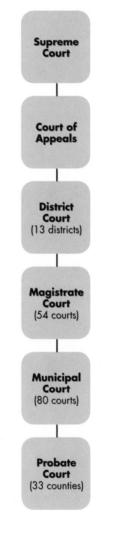

Supreme Court

Court of Appeals

District Court (13 districts)

Magistrate Court (54 courts)

Municipal Court (80 courts)

Probate Court (33 counties)

the judges who serve in the judiciary. Municipal courts deal with people who break local laws. Magistrate courts handle cases involving small debts or legal claims. The state's 13 district courts hear cases appealed from these lower courts. They also handle criminal cases and larger civil suits. If someone thinks a district court made an error, he or she can ask the seven judges on the court of appeals to review the case.

The most powerful court in New Mexico is the supreme court. Its five judges, called justices, serve eight-year terms. The supreme court hears cases from the lower courts. It also decides if laws follow New Mexico's **constitution**.

WORD TO KNOW

constitution *a written document that contains all the governing principles of a state or country*

New Mexico Counties

This map shows the 33 counties in New Mexico. Santa Fe, the state capital, is indicated with a star.

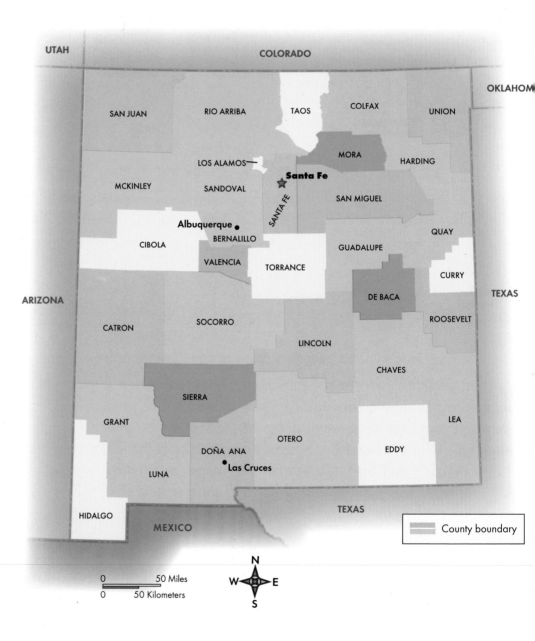

GOVERNMENT CLOSER TO HOME

New Mexico is divided into 33 counties, each with its own government. Voters elect county commissioners, who act as both a mini-legislature and executives. Voters also elect a treasurer, sheriff, assessor, probate judge, and clerk. A county manager helps carry out the commission's policies. Within each county are various cities, towns, and villages. Local and county governments build schools and libraries, hire police officers, and provide other essential public services.

New Mexico also has another kind of local government. By U.S. law, each Native American tribe is considered an independent nation. Voters on each pueblo and reservation choose a tribal president and council. These officials make business decisions for the nations and provide essential services. New Mexico's Indian Affairs Department works with the tribal governments to provide services the tribes can't afford on their own, such as building roads or stringing up power lines in remote areas. As U.S. citizens, Native Americans can vote in all state and national elections.

MINI-BIO

JOE GARCIA: RECLAIMING A NAME

For years, Joe Garcia (1953–) worked as an engineer at New Mexico's Los Alamos National Laboratory. A member of the San Juan Pueblo, he became involved in village politics in 1991. He first served as lieutenant governor and then became governor in 1995. Ten years later, he was governor for a second term when he made an important announcement for his people. The pueblo wanted to be known by its original name: Ohkay Owingeh. This Tewa language phrase means "place of strong people." San Juan was the name Spanish explorer Juan de Oñate had given the pueblo almost 400 years before.

? Want to know more? Visit www.factsfornow.scholastic.com and enter the keywords **New Mexico**.

State Flag

The first flag for New Mexico showed a small U.S. flag in one corner, the state seal in another, and the words *New Mexico*, all on a blue background. In 1920, some New Mexicans called for a new flag that would reflect the state's history. The resulting flag, introduced in 1925, is still used today. It shows a modern version of an old Zia symbol for the sun, with red rays pointing in four directions. The Zias considered the number four holy, because so many things come in fours—the main directions on a compass, the four seasons, and the four main stages of a person's life: childhood, youth, adulthood, and old age.

State Seal

New Mexico's first official seal was created after it became a U.S. territory in 1851. This seal showed an American eagle holding an olive branch in one claw and three arrows in the other. About 10 years later, a new seal showed a bald eagle with its wings outstretched. Underneath the wings was a smaller Mexican eagle holding a snake in its beak. In its claw was a cactus. In 1882, a small banner was placed beneath the eagles. It carries the Latin phrase *Crescit Eundo*, which means "It grows as it goes." Those words became the state's motto after it joined the Union in 1912, and the territorial seal became the state seal in 1913.

READ ABOUT

A worker serves coffee at a café in Santa Fe.

CHAPTER EIGHT

ECONOMY

★

IN COLONIAL DAYS, MOST NEW MEX-ICANS WERE FARMERS. Today, some people still grow crops and raise sheep and cattle. But most New Mexicans work in other jobs. Some spend their days in gleaming labs researching and developing new products. Others build high-tech gadgets in modern factories. Some mine the earth, while others drill for oil and gas. And a large number of New Mexicans make sure the state's many visitors have a good time exploring the Land of Enchantment!

Farmers harvest chile peppers in New Mexico.

FARMING AND RANCHING

About 60 percent of the state's land is used for agriculture, and the biggest chunk of that is used for ranching. Raising cattle is big business in New Mexico, just as it was in the Old West. Cattle and dairy products are the state's top agricultural items. Many sheep are also raised in the state. The wool of the churro sheep is prized for its strength.

What Do New Mexicans Do?

This color-coded chart shows what industries New Mexicans work in.

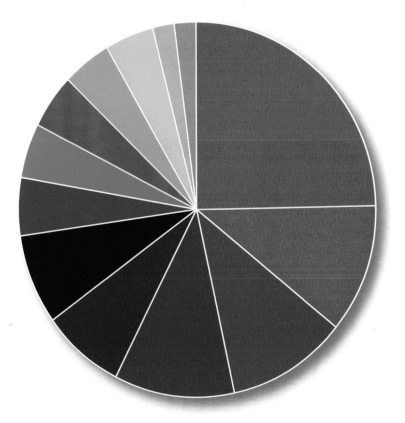

24.8% Educational services, and health care and social assistance 218,660

11.3% Retail trade 99,583

10.8% Professional, scientific, and management, and administrative and waste management services 95,640

10.6% Arts, entertainment, and recreation, and accommodation and food services 93,110

7.7% Public administration 67,904

7.6% Construction 66,690

5.1% Manufacturing 45,358

4.7% Finance and insurance, and real estate and rental and leasing 41,673

4.7% Other services, except public administration 41,430

4.5% Agriculture, forestry, fishing and hunting, and mining 39,457

4.4% Transportation and warehousing, and utilities 39,027

2.1% Wholesale trade 18,913

1.7% Information 15,016

Source: U.S. Census Bureau, 2010 census

New Mexico's top crops are hay, plants and flowers, and nuts. The nuts grown include pecans, pistachios, and piñons. Other important farm products are cotton and vegetables. The Ancestral Pueblos grew cotton centuries ago, and today New Mexican farmers sell millions of dollars worth of cotton every year. The most famous New Mexican vegetables are chiles. They come in different sizes and spiciness—from mild to mouth-burning!

MINI-BIO

ROY NAKAYAMA: THE CHILE MAN

Roy Nakayama (1923–1988) grew up on a farm in the Mesilla Valley of New Mexico. He stayed in the state almost his entire life and helped make the chile pepper a popular vegetable. Working as a plant scientist at New Mexico State University, he created new types of peppers. In 1975, he came up with one he called NuMex Big Jim. The pepper was almost 8 inches (20 cm) long, and it won a place in the *Guinness Book of World Records* as the biggest pepper ever! Nakayama also bred peppers that weren't too spicy, making them popular with backyard gardeners. For his efforts, he was sometimes called "the chile man."

 Want to know more? Visit www.factsfornow.scholastic.com and enter the keywords **New Mexico**.

Major Agricultural and Mining Products

This map shows where New Mexico's major agricultural and mining products come from. See a red and black drop? That means oil is found there.

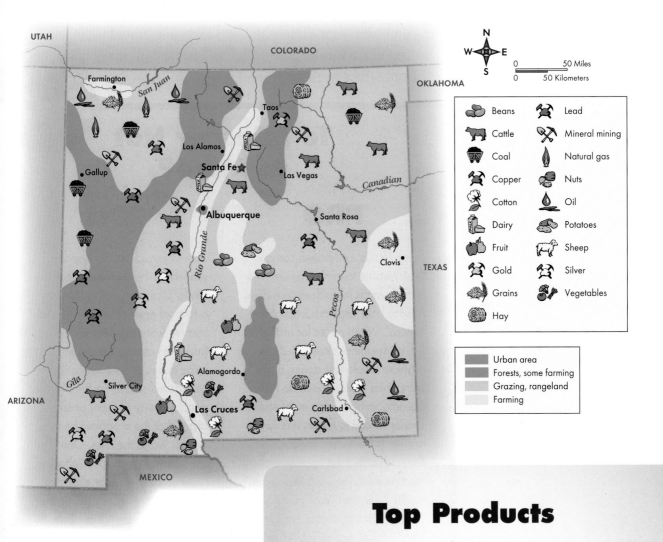

Legend:
- Beans
- Cattle
- Coal
- Copper
- Cotton
- Dairy
- Fruit
- Gold
- Grains
- Hay
- Lead
- Mineral mining
- Natural gas
- Nuts
- Oil
- Potatoes
- Sheep
- Silver
- Vegetables

- Urban area
- Forests, some farming
- Grazing, rangeland
- Farming

Top Products

Agriculture Cattle, dairy products, hay, pecans, peppers

Manufacturing Computers and electronic products, food products, chemical and fabricated metal products

Mining Coal, natural gas, oil, copper, sand and gravel, potash

New Mexico produces more potash than any other U.S. state.

WEALTH FROM THE EARTH

Mining ores and removing other valuable resources from the ground keep tens of thousands of New Mexicans working. Coal, which is burned to create electricity, is the number-one mineral in New Mexico. The state also produces copper, potash (used to make glass, fertilizer, and some medicines), and sand and gravel for construction. Smaller amounts of gold and silver are also mined.

THINK ABOUT IT!

To Mine or Not to Mine?

PRO

In the 1940s, companies came to New Mexico to mine uranium. The Navajo lands in northwestern New Mexico hold large amounts of the mineral. When prices for uranium fell, all the mines closed. But now uranium is valuable again, and companies want to return to New Mexico. Some leaders in the state support efforts to restart uranium mining in the Mount Taylor area. They argue that the operation offers much-needed jobs and tax money. In 2013, Grants/Cibola County Chamber of Commerce president Terry Fletcher explained, "I think the community feels there [have] been enough technology advancements in the last 30 years. It is something that can be done safely."

CON

Some Navajo people oppose reopening the mines on their lands. Uranium mining releases a form of energy called radiation into the water and the air. Radiation can be deadly in large doses. Mount Taylor is also considered sacred by the Navajo people. Many of these people argue that the economic benefits are not worth the risks. One Navajo woman, Jackie Jefferson, grew up playing near drainage ditches by the old uranium mine. In 2013, she said, "We don't want to be a dumping ground."

Thousands of oil and gas wells are scattered across New Mexico. Most of New Mexico's oil is pumped in the southeast corner of the state, while gas is most plentiful in the northwest corner.

MAKING GREAT THINGS

New companies spring up, requiring offices or warehouses. People moving into the state need homes. More homes and more people mean more services are needed. This also means a boom for the construction industry.

New Mexico has taken part in the high-tech boom since the 1970s. Major advances in electronics, lasers, and other high-tech fields have come from the Sandia and Los Alamos National Laboratories. The University of New Mexico and other state schools also carry out important research in science and technology. Intel, a private company, makes the silicon chips that power computers. It employs thousands of workers at its Rio Rancho plant north of Albuquerque. Many smaller companies also provide jobs making electronic devices.

LOOKING TO THE SKIES

A dry climate and open spaces drew rocket inventor Robert Goddard to New Mexico in the 1930s. Today, those same conditions help New Mexico attract jobs tied to **aviation** and spaceflight. The U.S. government performs research into rockets at the White Sands Missile Range. The government also has three air force bases in New Mexico. Together, they provide New Mexicans with tens of thousands of jobs. Near Socorro, the government operates the Very Large Array, a field of 27 huge satellite dishes. The satellites detect objects in space.

When Eclipse Aviation (now called Eclipse Aerospace) opened, New Mexico entered the field of aircraft manu-

FAQ

Q: **WHAT IS A WIND FARM?**

A: New Mexico is increasingly turning to wind power for its energy needs. To harness the wind, wind farms are built. A wind farm is a group of wind turbines that convert the power of the wind into electricity as they turn. New Mexico wind farms now provide power to more than 275,000 homes. In 2013, wind power accounted for 6.1 percent of the state's electricity. The state had 11 wind projects and 575 wind turbines in operation.

WORD TO KNOW

aviation *the design and manufacture of airplanes*

CHERYL WILLMAN: SEEKING A CURE

In her lab, Cheryl Willman (1954–) peers through microscopes and looks at test results. For more than 25 years, she has sought a cure for leukemia, a form of cancer. As a college student in Minnesota, she had thought about becoming a lawyer. But she turned to medicine because of her grandmother, who had wanted to be a doctor but never had the chance. Willman is now head of the Cancer Research and Treatment Center at the University of New Mexico. The work she and other doctors have done there has made the center one of the best in the country. She once saw patients on a regular basis. However, she felt that she could have a far greater impact on a greater number of people through research.

? Want to know more? Visit www.factsfornow.scholastic.com and enter the keywords **New Mexico**.

facturing. In 2006, the company delivered its first jet. Each of Eclipse's planes carries six passengers and is intended for small businesses. The Eclipse jet is lighter and less costly than other planes its size.

Spaceport America takes passengers even higher in the sky. The port, near the tiny town of Truth or Consequences, is the world's first center devoted to space travel for businesses and tourists. After its first successful launch in 2007, the state-run, taxpayer-funded Spaceport America opened officially in 2011. "Regular" people, not only trained astronauts, may soon be able to take rides into space.

SERVICES OF ALL KINDS

Banking, selling goods, government work, and health care are just some parts of New Mexico's service economy. When it comes to putting people to work, the government leads the way. Almost 200,000 people work for some level of government—local, county, state, federal, or tribal. The U.S. government is the largest employer in the state.

Another service involves taking care of the more than 30 million tourists who visit New Mexico each year. Those guests spend more than $5 billion, keeping tour guides, chefs, hotel workers, and others in the tourism industry on their toes.

Visitors also spend money at New Mexico pueblos and reservations. Some visitors want to learn about Native American history. Some visit pueblo casinos, resort hotels, and golf courses. Tourism brings income to the Native nations.

Visitors enjoy a performance by Zuni Pueblo dancers at the Bandelier National Monument.

MINI-BIO

CONRAD HILTON: A HOTEL FAMILY

As a boy in San Antonio, New Mexico, Conrad Hilton (1887–1979) watched his parents turn their home into a small inn. Guests paid a dollar a night for a clean room and a meal. As a young man, Hilton went to Texas and bought a hotel. Soon he owned several more, and one that opened in 1925 was the first to carry his name. Starting in the 1950s, he built a chain of Hilton hotels across the United States and overseas. Today, the Hilton Hotels Corporation has business ties to thousands of hotels.

? **Want to know more?** Visit www.factsfor now.scholastic.com and enter the keywords **New Mexico**.

CHAPTER NINE

TRAVEL GUIDE

⭐

ALMOST ANYWHERE YOU LOOK IN NEW MEXICO, THERE'S SOME-THING FASCINATING TO SEE. The natural wonders include mountains, the remains of volcanoes, and beautiful rock for-mations. New Mexicans have built museums and attractions and spent money to improve their cities to cater to millions of visitors each year. Let's take a look at some of what New Mexico has to offer!

←—Follow along with this travel map. We'll begin in Shiprock and travel all the way down to Carlsbad.

NORTH-WESTERN

THINGS TO DO: Explore Ancestral Pueblo ruins, visit a city in the sky, and shiver in an ice cave.

Shiprock

★ **Shiprock:** The town and the rock share the same name. Some 19th-century soldiers thought the massive rock looked like a grand sailing ship, leading to the name. The Navajo believed Shiprock was once a giant bird. Scientists say the rock, which rises more than 1,400 feet (430 m) above the surrounding plain, is around 30 million years old.

Shiprock

Nageezi

★ **Chaco Culture National Historical Park:** The most spectacular remains of the Ancestral Pueblo people in New Mexico are at Chaco Canyon. After bouncing over dirt roads, you come to the massive Pueblo Bonito and the rest of the ruins of what was once a great city. For a real adventure, walk the trails in remote parts of the park.

Aztec

★ **Aztec Ruins National Monument:** The pueblo here once had more than 400 rooms. A massive kiva at the site has been rebuilt for visitors to explore. Inside, you can hear recordings of Native American music.

Zuni

★ **Zuni Pueblo:** To the Spanish, the original Zuni pueblo was part of the legendary Seven Cities of Cíbola. Today, Zuni Pueblo is home to more than 10,000 people, making it the largest pueblo in New Mexico. The residents are happy to show you their art and some of their traditional dances.

The roof of the original Great Kiva at Aztec Ruins National Monument was thought to have weighed 90 tons.

SEE IT HERE!

SKY CITY

The people of Acoma didn't welcome the early Spanish explorers who wanted to enter their pueblo. But things have changed over the centuries, and now tourists can explore the "Sky City" of the Acomas. The city offers guided tours, a museum, and a cultural center dedicated to preserving Acoma history and traditions.

Acoma pottery

Ramah

★ **El Morro National Monument:** A pool of water in the middle of desert country made El Morro a popular spot for travelers of old. Today, only animals drink from the pool, but visitors can see the words that humans carved into nearby rocks hundreds of years ago.

Grants

★ **Ice Cave & Bandera Volcano:** Here's a cool way to get some relief on a hot day—explore a cave of ice! A tube of hardened lava leads down to the cave, where the temperature never goes above 31°F (–1°C).

★ **El Malpais National Monument:** You'll see lava flows, ancient ruins, and historic homesteads at this site of prehistoric volcanoes.

La Ventana Natural Arch at El Malpais National Monument

NORTH-EASTERN NEW MEXICO

THINGS TO DO: Dive into the Blue Hole, stroll the streets where gunslingers once walked, and learn more about New Mexico's Rough Riders.

Las Vegas

★ **City of Las Vegas Museum & Rough Rider Memorial Collection:** The area around Las Vegas was home to many of the Rough Riders who served under Teddy Roosevelt during the Spanish-American War. The Rough Rider Memorial honors those brave New Mexicans and the future president who led them.

Cimarron

★ **Old Town:** Walk past the original buildings in the heart of Cimarron and you can almost smell the gunpowder and horses. A walking tour here includes 14 historic buildings.

Scuba school at the Blue Hole

Santa Rosa

★ **Blue Hole:** It's hard to believe, but you can find a scuba-diving paradise in the middle of this dry state. The Blue Hole is 80 feet (24 m) deep and carved out of sandstone. The crystal-clear waters are 64°F (18°C) all year.

★ **Vermejo Park Ranch:** Covering an area almost as big as Rhode Island, this ranch is owned by Ted Turner, founder of Cable News Network (CNN). Guests come to see bear, bison, and other animals living in the wild.

Capulin

★ **Capulin Volcano National Monument:** Ever wanted to walk inside a volcano? Then head to Capulin. The volcano here erupted about 60,000 years ago. It is no longer active, so you can safely explore inside the volcano and walk along its rim.

NORTH-CENTRAL NEW MEXICO

THINGS TO DO: Explore ancient ruins, soar over Albuquerque, and learn about Hispanic culture.

Albuquerque

★ **New Mexico Museum of Natural History and Science:** At the museum, you can explore more than 4 billion years of New Mexico history. As you enter, say hello to Spike and Alberta, dinosaur skeletons that stand on either side of the door. Inside, you can learn more about volcanoes and explore the stars in the museum's planetarium.

An art exhibit at the National Hispanic Cultural Center

★ **National Hispanic Cultural Center:** Located in a traditionally Hispanic neighborhood, the cultural center promotes the study of everything Hispanic. It features art exhibits, musical performances, talks on Spanish-language literature, and Spanish language lessons.

★ **Indian Pueblo Cultural Center:** The 19 Pueblo groups of New Mexico own and operate this center, which features historic as well as contemporary art and **artifacts** from the pueblos.

WORD TO KNOW

artifacts *items created by humans, usually for a practical purpose*

New Mexico Museum of Natural History and Science

MINI-BIO

J. PAUL TAYLOR: THE MAN FROM MESILLA

J. Paul Taylor (1920–) has lived in the village of Mesilla for more than 60 years. He and his wife raised their seven children in an adobe house full of folk art, ceramics, quilts, Hopi and Navajo blankets, and Spanish and South American artwork. Taylor worked as a teacher and principal for three decades. "[As an educator,] I wanted to teach New Mexican history differently," he explains. "I wanted my students to see and touch their history. To understand the connection between their lives now and their past." Later, Taylor served in the state legislature, where he was known as an advocate for arts and culture. In 2003, the Taylor family donated their historic home and two storefronts to the Museum of New Mexico as a state monument.

? Want to know more? Visit www.factsfornowscholastic.com and enter the keywords **New Mexico**.

★ **Petroglyph National Monument:** This site on the western edge of Albuquerque offers a glimpse into the Pueblos' past. Here, Native Americans left thousands of carvings in the rocks made 400 to 700 years ago.

Hikers at Sandia Peak

★ **Sandia Peak:** Located just northeast of Albuquerque, Sandia Peak is a 10,378-foot (3,163 m) mountain that's popular with skiers and snowboarders. Tourists can go partway up the mountain on a **tram** for a bird's-eye view of the region.

WORD TO KNOW

tram *a carrier that travels on overhead rails or cables*

Taos

★ **Taos Pueblo:** The pueblo has been continually occupied for nearly 1,000 years. Here visitors can learn about Pueblo history and explore ancient Pueblo buildings.

★ **Kit Carson Home and Museum:** The one-time frontier scout bought this home near the Taos Plaza as a wedding gift for his wife. Now you can walk the same wooden floors that Kit and his family used. Two other homes nearby serve as the museum, which offers a glimpse into Taos's past.

Taos Ski Valley

Taos Pueblo

★ **Taos Ski Valley:** If gliding down powdery slopes is your thing, Taos Ski Valley is a must-see. Located about 20 miles (30 km) outside of Taos, the ski area has some of the toughest trails in the country.

Chama

★ **Cumbres and Toltec Scenic Railroad:** All aboard! A steam train takes visitors over the same route once used to haul silver and other minerals through the Rocky Mountains. The railroad is a "movie star," too—several films have scenes that were shot along the mountain route!

Santa Fe

★ **Palace of the Governors:** Spanish, Mexican, and American officials have all worked within the adobe walls of the Palace of the Governors. Now it features exhibits on New Mexico's multicultural past.

★ **New Mexico History Museum:** Visit one of the state's newest museums, right next to its oldest—the Palace of the Governors. The New Mexico History Museum opened in 2009 and offers exhibitions about the state's early indigenous people, Spanish colonists, the Mexican era, Santa Fe Trail riders, and the railroad.

★ **Georgia O'Keeffe Museum:** Also next door to the Palace of the Governors is a museum dedicated to one of America's finest painters,

Spiral staircase at Loretto Chapel

Georgia O'Keeffe. The museum owns some of O'Keeffe's best-known works and also displays items on loan from other art collections.

★ **Loretto Chapel:** A mystery swirls around the spiral staircase that makes this 1873 chapel unique. The stairs make two full turns as they go up, and nothing supports them. The staircase is held together without any screws or nails.

★ **Museum Hill:** Four museums sit on this spot, just southeast of the center of Santa Fe. The Museum of International Folk Art displays work from more than 100 countries. The art and history of New

Native American crafts for sale at the Palace of the Governors

Mexico's Native people is featured at the Museum of Indian Arts and Culture. The Wheelwright Museum of the American Indian has modern Native American art from across the Southwest. And the Museum of Spanish Colonial Art, the newest museum on the hill, shows the skills of the Spanish-speaking settlers who lived in New Mexico during the 18th and 19th centuries.

★ **The Roundhouse:** A trip to the Roundhouse lets you see how government operates in New Mexico. The state capitol has self-guided tours, and its beautiful grounds feature many kinds of plants and trees.

SEE IT HERE!

EL RANCHO DE LAS GOLONDRINAS

To step back in time to colonial New Mexico, head out of Santa Fe to this ranch. It is a "living" museum with actual buildings from 18th-century farms. Some have always been on the site, while others were moved there from elsewhere in northern New Mexico. Actors dressed in period clothes show how settlers lived on the frontier of colonial Spain.

Los Alamos

★ **Bandelier National Monument:** Climb into cliff dwellings that were once the home of Pueblo people at Bandelier. The site also has pueblo ruins and more than 70 miles (110 km) of hiking trails.

★ **Bradbury Science Museum:** You can't visit the labs at the Los Alamos National Laboratory, but you can learn a little about what goes on there at its science museum. Located in downtown Los Alamos, the Bradbury has exhibits on nuclear weapons, lasers, and high-tech wonders.

Bradbury Science Museum

Pecos

★ **Pecos National Historical Park:**
As many as 2,000 Pueblo people
once lived here. When the Spanish
came, they built a large mission
church. Ruins from both the Pueblo
and the Spanish are yours to explore.

SOUTH-WESTERN

THINGS TO DO: Take a
refreshing dip in the hot
springs, learn about some very large "dishes" in
Socorro, and explore the cave dwellings of the
Mogollon people.

Las Cruces

★ **New Mexico Farm and Ranch
Heritage Museum:** New Mexico
State University hosts this museum
that honors the state's farming and
ranching history. The museum is
also a working farm, where you can
meet livestock and watch cows getting milked.

Socorro

★ **Very Large Array:** Satellite dishes
that bring TV shows into homes are
specks compared to the 27 dishes at
the Very Large Array. Each one is
82 feet (25 m) wide and weighs 235
tons! Stop by and learn more about
how picking up radio waves from
space helps scientists learn about
the universe.

A satellite dish in the Very Large Array

Mineral Hot Springs

Truth or Consequences

★ **Mineral Hot Springs:** Long before white settlers came to New Mexico, Native Americans soothed aches and pains in the waters of the hot springs here. The mineral-filled water bubbles up from under the ground.

Silver City

★ **Gila Cliff Dwellings National Monument:** Not much has changed in the cliffs since the Mogollon people lived there more than 700 years ago. Visitors can explore rooms that were once part of a Mogollon village.

Visitors at Gila Cliff Dwellings National Monument

FAQ ★ ★ ★

Q8 HOW DID TRUTH OR CONSEQUENCES, NEW MEXICO, GET ITS NAME?

A8 In 1950, *Truth or Consequences* was the name of a popular radio show (later it was also on television). The show's producers said it would broadcast live from any town that changed its name to Truth or Consequences. The residents of Hot Springs went along with the offer. Today, the town is also sometimes called T or C.

SOUTH-EASTERN NEW MEXICO

THINGS TO DO: Learn about UFOs (unidentified flying objects), slide down white sand dunes, and see hundreds of thousands of bats.

Alamogordo

★ **New Mexico Museum of Space History:** Scientists in New Mexico have played a big part in space exploration. Learn more about their achievements at the state's museum of space history. The museum is also home to the International Space Hall of Fame.

★ **White Sands National Monument:** It's been said that White Sands is like no other place on Earth. Many visitors are stunned by this huge stretch of whiteness, which constantly shifts with the wind. Hiking, bird-watching, and biking are popular activities at the monument.

White Sands National Monument

SEE IT HERE!

ALIENS AMONG US?

Want to find out more about UFOs? Then Roswell is the place to go—it's the home of the International UFO Museum! In 1947, residents around Roswell thought they saw a "flying saucer," or UFO. At first, the U.S. government reported it was a UFO, but then officials said it was just a weather balloon. Whatever it was, Roswell became a center for people who believe that UFOs and space aliens are real.

International UFO Museum

Fort Sumner

★ **Old Fort Sumner Museum and Cemetery:** Wild West outlaw Billy the Kid is buried at Old Fort Sumner. Near the museum is a monument that honors the memory of 19th-century Apaches and Navajos, who were forced to live at the fort before being moved to reservations.

SEE IT HERE!

WESTERN HERITAGE MUSEUM

Hobbs, near the Texas border, is the home of the Western Heritage Museum. The museum is filled with information about the cowboys and ranchers who once lived in New Mexico and across the Southwest. It also houses the Lea County Cowboy Hall of Fame. The region around Hobbs claims more world-champion rodeo cowboys than any other part of the world.

Carlsbad

★ **Living Desert Zoo and Gardens State Park:** Mountain lions, rattle-snakes, bears, and more can be seen at this park, where injured wild animals are taken to heal before going back into the wild. The park also has many kinds of cacti and other desert plants.

★ **Carlsbad Caverns National Park:** Watch bats soar off for their evening meals, or get your hands dirty on a cave tour. These are just two of the fun events waiting at Carlsbad Caverns. In the underground caves, the temperature is always a cool 56°F (13°C).

WOW

A cave at Carlsbad Caverns called the **Big Room** is about the size of six football fields!

The Big Room at Carlsbad Caverns

WRITING PROJECTS

Check out these ideas for creating campaign brochures and writing you-are-there editorials. Or research famous New Mexicans.

118

ART PROJECTS

Create a great PowerPoint presentation, illustrate the state song, or research the state quarter and design your own.

119

TIMELINE

What happened when? This timeline highlights important events in the state's history—and shows what was happening throughout the United States at the same time.

122

GLOSSARY

Remember the Words to Know from the chapters in this book? They're all collected here.

125

FAST FACTS

Use this section to find fascinating facts about state symbols, land area and population statistics, weather, sports teams, and much more.

126

WRITING PROJECTS

Write a Memoir, Journal, or Editorial for Your School Newspaper!

Picture Yourself . . .

★ As a Native American, African American, or woman in early New Mexico, struggling to attain the full rights of citizenship, including the right to vote.

★ In your research, read about Miguel Trujillo and Adelina Otero-Warren.

★ Explain what reasons the government gave for denying certain groups their basic rights as citizens. What actions do you take to win the right to vote?

SEE: Chapter Four, pages 47–48, and Chapter Five, pages 57 and 62.

Create an Election Brochure or Web Site!

Run for office! Throughout this book, you've read about some of the issues that concern New Mexico today. As a candidate for governor of New Mexico, create a campaign brochure or Web site.

★ Explain how you meet the qualifications to be governor of New Mexico.

★ Talk about the three or four major issues you'll focus on if you're elected.

★ Remember, you'll be responsible for New Mexico's budget. How would you spend the taxpayers' money?

SEE: Chapter Seven, pages 85–86.

Create an interview script with a famous person from New Mexico!

★ Research various famous New Mexicans, such as Brian Urlacher, Nancy Lopez, Maria Martinez, and many others.

★ Based on your research, pick one person you would most like to interview.

★ Write a script of the interview. What questions would you ask? How would this famous person answer? Create a question-and-answer format. You may want to supplement this writing project with a voice-recording dramatization of the interview.

SEE: Chapter Six, pages 74–79, and the Biographical Dictionary, pages 133–137.

Nancy Lopez

ART PROJECTS

Illustrate the Lyrics to the New Mexico State Songs
("O Fair New Mexico" and "Así Es Nuevo Méjico")

Use markers, paints, photos, collages, colored pencils, or computer graphics to illustrate the lyrics to "O Fair New Mexico" and "Así Es Nuevo Méjico." Turn your illustrations into a picture book, or scan them into PowerPoint and add music.

SEE: The lyrics to both state songs on page 128.

Create a PowerPoint Presentation or Visitors' Guide
Welcome to New Mexico!

New Mexico is a great place to visit and to live! From its natural beauty to its bustling cities and historical sites, there's plenty to see and do. In your PowerPoint presentation or brochure, highlight 10 to 15 of New Mexico's fascinating landmarks. Be sure to include:

★ a map of the state showing where these sites are located

★ photos, illustrations, Web links, natural history facts, geographic stats, climate and weather, plants and wildlife, and recent discoveries

SEE: Chapter One, pages 9–21, and Chapter Nine, pages 103–115.

Research New Mexico's State Quarter

From 1999 to 2008, the U.S. Mint introduced new quarters commemorating each of the 50 states in the order that they were admitted to the Union. Each state's quarter features a unique design on its reverse, or back.

★ Research the significance of the image. Who designed the quarter? Who chose the final design?

★ Design your own New Mexico state quarter. What images would you choose for the reverse?

★ Make a poster showing the New Mexico quarter and label each image.

GO TO: www.factsfornow.scholastic.com. Enter the keywords **New Mexico** and look for the link to the New Mexico quarter.

SCIENCE, TECHNOLOGY, ENGINEERING, & MATH PROJECTS

Graph Population Statistics!

★ Compare population statistics (such as ethnic background, birth, death, and literacy rates) in New Mexico counties or major cities.

★ In your graph or chart, look at population density and write sentences describing what the population statistics show; graph one set of population statistics and write a paragraph explaining what the graphs reveal.

SEE: Chapter Six, pages 65–70.

Create a Weather Map of New Mexico!

Use your knowledge of New Mexico's geography to research and identify conditions that result in specific weather events. What is it about the geography of New Mexico that makes it vulnerable to droughts? Create a weather map or poster that shows the weather patterns over the state, or display wet and dry years between 1895 and the present. Include a caption explaining the technology used to measure weather phenomena such as droughts and provide data.

SEE: Chapter One, pages 17–18.

Mexican spotted owl

Track Endangered Species

Using your knowledge of New Mexico's wildlife, research which animals and plants are endangered or threatened.

★ Find out what the state is doing to protect these species.

★ Chart known populations of the animals and plants, and report on changes in certain geographic areas.

SEE: Chapter One, page 21.

PRIMARY VS. SECONDARY SOURCES

What's the Diff?

Your teacher may require at least one or two primary sources and one or two secondary sources for your assignment. So, what's the difference between the two?

★ **Primary sources are original.** You are reading the actual words of someone's diary, journal, letter, autobiography, or interview. Primary sources can also be photographs, maps, prints, cartoons, news/film footage, posters, first-person newspaper articles, drawings, musical scores, and recordings. By the way, when you conduct a survey, interview someone, shoot a video, or take photographs to include in a project, you are creating primary sources!

★ **Secondary sources are what you find in encyclopedias, textbooks, articles, biographies, and almanacs.** These are written by a person or group of people who tell about something that happened to someone else. Secondary sources also recount what another person said or did. This book is an example of a secondary source.

Now that you know what primary sources are—where can you find them?

★ **Your school or local library:** Check the library catalog for collections of original writings, government documents, musical scores, and so on. Some of this material may be stored on microfilm.

★ **Historical societies:** These organizations keep historical documents, photographs, and other materials. Staff members can help you find what you are looking for. History museums are also great places to see primary sources firsthand.

★ **The Internet:** There are lots of sites that have primary sources you can download and use in a project or assignment.

TIMELINE

★ ★ ★

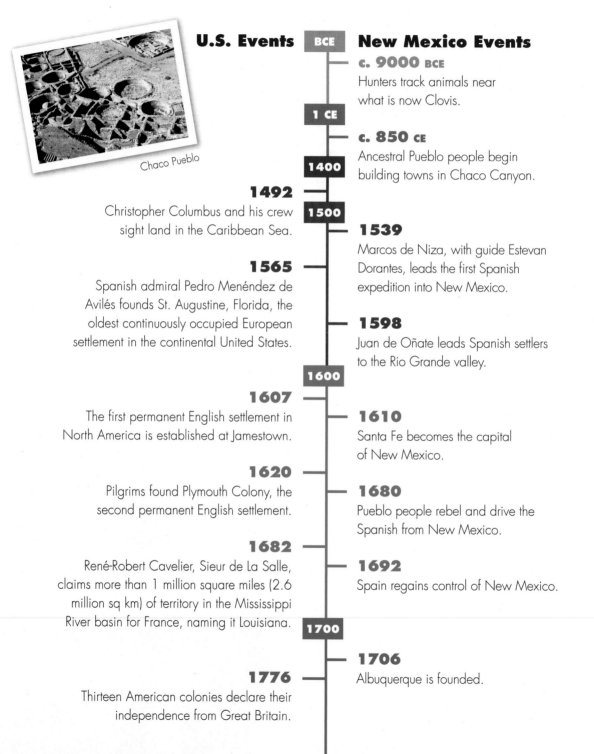

Chaco Pueblo

U.S. Events

BCE

1 CE

1400

1492
Christopher Columbus and his crew sight land in the Caribbean Sea.

1500

1565
Spanish admiral Pedro Menéndez de Avilés founds St. Augustine, Florida, the oldest continuously occupied European settlement in the continental United States.

1600

1607
The first permanent English settlement in North America is established at Jamestown.

1620
Pilgrims found Plymouth Colony, the second permanent English settlement.

1682
René-Robert Cavelier, Sieur de La Salle, claims more than 1 million square miles (2.6 million sq km) of territory in the Mississippi River basin for France, naming it Louisiana.

1700

1776
Thirteen American colonies declare their independence from Great Britain.

New Mexico Events

c. 9000 BCE
Hunters track animals near what is now Clovis.

c. 850 CE
Ancestral Pueblo people begin building towns in Chaco Canyon.

1539
Marcos de Niza, with guide Estevan Dorantes, leads the first Spanish expedition into New Mexico.

1598
Juan de Oñate leads Spanish settlers to the Rio Grande valley.

1610
Santa Fe becomes the capital of New Mexico.

1680
Pueblo people rebel and drive the Spanish from New Mexico.

1692
Spain regains control of New Mexico.

1706
Albuquerque is founded.

U.S. Events

1787
The U.S. Constitution is written.

1800

1803
The Louisiana Purchase almost doubles the size of the United States.

1830
The Indian Removal Act forces eastern Native American groups to relocate west of the Mississippi River.

1846–48
The United States fights a war with Mexico over western territories in the Mexican War.

The capture of Santa Fe

1861–65
The American Civil War is fought between the Northern Union and the Southern Confederacy; it ends with the surrender of the Confederate army, led by General Robert E. Lee.

1886
Apache leader Geronimo surrenders to the U.S. Army, ending the last major Native American rebellion against the expansion of the United States into the West.

1898
The United States gains control of Puerto Rico, the Philippines, and Guam after defeating Spain in the Spanish-American War.

New Mexico Events

1821
New Mexico becomes part of the independent nation of Mexico; William Becknell opens the Santa Fe Trail.

1846
U.S. forces invade New Mexico and eventually take it from Spain.

1850
New Mexico becomes a U.S. territory.

1853
The Gadsden Purchase adds some Mexican lands to New Mexico.

1862
Union and Confederate forces battle at Glorieta Pass during the Civil War.

1868
The Navajos agree to end raids of white settlements and move to a reservation.

1878
Fighting between ranchers and merchants erupts in Lincoln County.

1898
Hundreds of New Mexicans volunteer to serve as Rough Riders in the Spanish-American War.

U.S. Events `1900` **New Mexico Events**

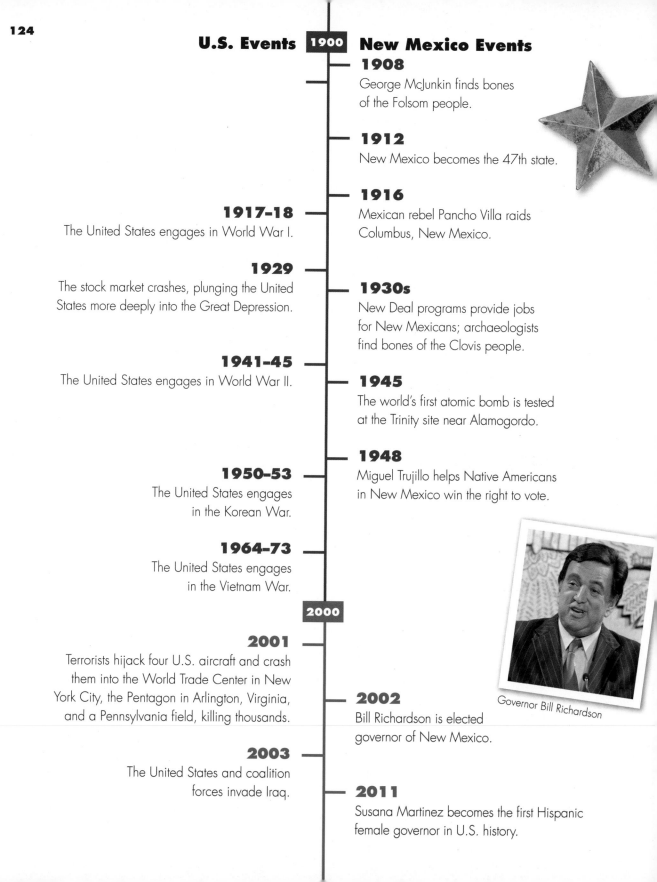

1908
George McJunkin finds bones
of the Folsom people.

1912
New Mexico becomes the 47th state.

1916
Mexican rebel Pancho Villa raids
Columbus, New Mexico.

1917–18
The United States engages in World War I.

1929
The stock market crashes, plunging the United
States more deeply into the Great Depression.

1930s
New Deal programs provide jobs
for New Mexicans; archaeologists
find bones of the Clovis people.

1941–45
The United States engages in World War II.

1945
The world's first atomic bomb is tested
at the Trinity site near Alamogordo.

1948
Miguel Trujillo helps Native Americans
in New Mexico win the right to vote.

1950–53
The United States engages
in the Korean War.

1964–73
The United States engages
in the Vietnam War.

`2000`

2001
Terrorists hijack four U.S. aircraft and crash
them into the World Trade Center in New
York City, the Pentagon in Arlington, Virginia,
and a Pennsylvania field, killing thousands.

2002
Bill Richardson is elected
governor of New Mexico.

Governor Bill Richardson

2003
The United States and coalition
forces invade Iraq.

2011
Susana Martinez becomes the first Hispanic
female governor in U.S. history.

GLOSSARY

★ ★ ★

abolished put an end to

ancestral relating to an ancestor, or a family member from the distant past

archaeologists people who study the remains of past human societies

artifacts items created by humans, usually for a practical purpose

aviation the design and manufacture of airplanes

cavalry soldiers who ride on horseback

constitution a written document that contains all the governing principles of a state or country

endangered in danger of becoming extinct

erosion the gradual wearing away of rock or soil by physical breakdown, chemical solution, or water

fossils the remains or prints of ancient animals or plants left in stone

friar a member of a men's Roman Catholic group who teaches about Christianity

gorge a narrow, steep-walled canyon

missionaries people who try to convert others to a religion

petition a list of voters' signatures requesting some action

petrified changed into a stony hardness

plateau an elevated part of the earth with steep slopes

prejudiced having an unreasonable hatred or fear of others

reservoirs artificial lakes or tanks created for water storage

semiarid receiving 10 to 20 inches (25 to 50 cm) of rain every year

suffrage the right to vote

threatened likely to become endangered in the foreseeable future

tram a carrier that travels on overhead rails or cables

undocumented lacking documents required for legal immigration or residence

FAST FACTS

★ ★ ★

State Symbols

State seal

Statehood date	January 6, 1912, the 47th state
Origin of state name	From the Spanish name La Nueva Mexico, which in English is "New Mexico"
State capital	Santa Fe
State nickname	The Land of Enchantment
State motto	*Crescit Eundo* ("It grows as it goes")
State bird	Roadrunner
State flower	Yucca
State animal	Black bear
State fish	Cutthroat trout
State fossil	*Coelophysis*
State gem	Turquoise
State insect	Tarantula Hawk Wasp
State songs	"*Así Es Nuevo Méjico*" and "O Fair New Mexico"
State grass	Blue grama
State tree	Piñon, or nut pine
State fair	Albuquerque (mid-September)

Geography

Total area; rank	121,590 square miles (314,919 sq km); 5th
Land; rank	121,297 square miles (314,159 sq km); 5th
Water; rank	293 square miles (759 sq km); 49th
Inland water; rank	293 square miles (759 sq km); 45th
Geographic center	Torrance County, 12 miles (19 km) southwest of Willard
Latitude	31°20' N to 37° N
Longitude	103° W to 109° W
Highest point	Wheeler Peak, 13,161 feet (4,011 m)
Lowest point	Red Bluff Reservoir, 2,842 feet (866 m)
Largest city	Albuquerque
Number of counties	33
Longest river	Rio Grande

Population

Population; rank (2010 census)	2,059,179; 36th
Density (2010 census)	17 persons per square mile (7 per sq km)
Population distribution (2010 census)	77% urban, 23% rural
Ethnic distribution (2010 census)	Persons of Hispanic or Latino origin: 46.3%
	White persons: 40.5%
	American Indian and Alaska Native persons: 8.5%
	Black persons: 1.7%
	Persons reporting two or more races: 1.4%
	Asian persons: 1.3%
	Persons of some other race: 0.2%
	Native Hawaiian and other Pacific Islander: 0.1%

Weather

Record high temperature	122°F (50°C) at Waste Isolation Pilot Plant, near Carlsbad, on June 27, 1994
Record low temperature	−50°F (−46°C) at Gavilan, near Lindrith, on February 1, 1951
Average July temperature, Albuquerque	78°F (26°C)
Average January temperature, Albuquerque	36°F (2°C)
Average annual precipitation, Albuquerque	9 inches (23 cm)

State flag

STATE SONGS

★ ★ ★

New Mexico has two state songs, one in English and one in Spanish. "O Fair New Mexico," words and music by Elizabeth Garrett, was adopted in 1917. "Así Es Nuevo Méjico," words and music by Amadeo Lucero, was adopted in 1971.

"O Fair New Mexico"

Under a sky of azure, where balmy breezes blow,
Kissed by the golden sunshine, is Nuevo Méjico.
Home of the Montezuma, with fiery heart aglow,
State of the deeds historic, is Nuevo Méjico.

Chorus:
O fair New Mexico, we love, we love you so,
Our hearts with pride o'erflow, no matter where
    we go,
O fair New Mexico, we love you, we love you so,
The grandest state to know, New Mexico.

(Chorus)
Rugged and high sierras, with deep canyons below,
Dotted with fertile valleys, is Nuevo Méjico.
Fields full of sweet alfalfa, richest perfumes bestow,
State of apple blossoms, is Nuevo Méjico.

(Chorus)
Days that are full of heart-dreams, nights when the
    moon hangs low,
Beaming its benediction, o'er Nuevo Méjico.
Land with its bright mañana [tomorrow], coming
    through weal and woe,
State of our esperanza [hope] is Nuevo Méjico.

"Así Es Nuevo Méjico"

Un canto que traigo muy dentro del alma
Lo canto a mi estado, mi tierra natal.
De flores dorada mi tierra encantada
De lindas mujeres, que no tiene igual.

Chorus:
Así es Nuevo Méjico
Así es esta tierra del sol
De sierras y valles, de tierras frutales
Así es Nuevo Méjico.
El negro, el hispano, el anglo, y el indio,
todos son tus hijos, todos por igual.
Tus pueblos, y aldeas, mi tierra encantada
De lindas mujeres que no tiene igual.

(Chorus)
El Río del Norte que es el Río Grande
Sus aguas corrientes fluyen hasta el mar,
Y riegan tus campos
Mi tierra encantada de lindas mujeres
Que no tiene igual.

(Chorus)
Tus campos se visten de flores de mayo,
De lindos colores que Diós les dotó
Tus pájaros cantan, mi tierra encantada,
Sus trinos de amores al ser celestial.

(Chorus)
Mi tierra encantada de historia bañada
Tan linda, tan bella, sin comparación.
Te rindo homenaje, te rindo cariño
Soldado valiente, te rinde su amor.

For the English translation, see http://en.wikipedia.org/wiki/Asi_Es_Nuevo_México

NATURAL AREAS AND HISTORIC SITES

★ ★ ★

National Park

Carlsbad Caverns National Park, the state's only national park, features a series of connected caverns and has one of the world's largest underground spaces.

National Monuments

New Mexico features 10 national monuments, including *Aztec Ruins National Monument*; *Bandelier National Monument*; *Capulin Volcano National Monument*; *El Malpais National Monument*; *El Morro National Monument*; *Fort Union National Monument*; *Gila Cliff Dwellings National Monument*; *Petroglyph National Monument*; *Salinas Pueblo Missions National Monument*; *White Sands National Monument*.

National Historical Parks

Chaco Culture National Historical Park, the site of a major urban center of ancestral Puebloan cultures, preserves some of the finest ancient structures in the United States.

The *Pecos National Historical Park* preserves 12,000 years of history, including the ancient pueblo of Pecos, two Spanish colonial missions, Santa Fe Trail sites, the site of the Civil War Battle of Glorieta Pass, and 20th-century ranch history.

National Historic Trails

El Camino Real de Tierra Adentro National Historic Trail is a trail that features more than 300 years of heritage and culture in the Southwest.

The *Old Spanish National Historic Trail* passes through six different states, linking Santa Fe to Los Angeles, California.

The *Santa Fe National Historic Trail* is another trail that passes through five states, linking Missouri to New Mexico.

State Parks and Forests

The New Mexico state park system maintains more than 30 state parks and recreation areas, including *Cimarron Canyon State Park*, *Oasis State Park*, *Rio Grande Nature Center State Park*, and *Ute Lake State Park*.

SPORTS TEAMS

★ ★ ★

NCAA Teams (Division I)

University of New Mexico *Lobos*
New Mexico State University *Aggies*

New Mexico State basketball players celebrating a win

CULTURAL INSTITUTIONS

★ ★ ★

Libraries

Albuquerque Public Library is the largest public library in the state.

The *New Mexico State Library* has been a leader in the development of New Mexico's public libraries, helping them to build the programs needed by their communities. The library features a Southwest special collections department.

Museums

The *Albuquerque Museum* (Albuquerque) has a fine collection of European and Native American art.

The *Bradbury Science Museum* (Los Alamos) shows the development of atomic energy.

El Rancho de las Golondrinas (Santa Fe) re-creates life among the Hispanic settlers of New Mexico in the early 1700s.

The *Museum of New Mexico* (Santa Fe) located in the Palace of the Governors includes the Museum of Fine Arts, the Museum of Indian Arts, and the Museum of International Folk Art.

The *Wheelwright Museum of the American Indian* (Santa Fe) hosts changing exhibitions of contemporary and historic Native American art with an emphasis on the Southwest.

Performing Arts

The *New Mexico Ballet Company* (Albuquerque), founded in 1972, is the oldest ballet company in New Mexico.

The *New Mexico Philharmonic* (Albuquerque) has been the state's major professional symphony orchestra since 2011.

Opera Southwest (Albuquerque), founded in 1972 as Albuquerque Opera Theatre, presents two or three major operas each year.

Universities and Colleges

In 2011, New Mexico had 8 public and 11 private institutions of higher learning.

ANNUAL EVENTS

January–March

King's Day Dances in several pueblos (January 6)

Winter Carnival in Red River (January)

Rio Grande Arts and Crafts Festival in Albuquerque (March)

April–June

Green Corn Dance at San Felipe Pueblo (May)

Rodeo de Santa Fe (June)

New Mexico Arts and Crafts Fair in Albuquerque (late June)

July–September

International Folk Art Market in Santa Fe (July)

"The Last Escape of Billy the Kid" Pageant in Lincoln (early August)

Inter-Tribal Indian Ceremonial in Gallup (August)

Santa Fe Indian Market (August)

Great American Duck Race in Deming (August)

Hatch Valley Chile Festival in Hatch (August)

All-American Futurity Horse Race in Ruidoso (September)

Whole Enchilada Fiesta in Las Cruces (September)

Fiesta de Santa Fe (mid-September)

New Mexico State Fair in Albuquerque (September)

October–December

Navajo Fair in Shiprock (October)

Taos Fall Arts Festival (September-October)

Albuquerque International Balloon Fiesta (October)

Winter Spanish Market in Santa Fe (November)

Red Rock Balloon Rally in Gallup (December)

Farolito Walk on Canyon Road in Santa Fe (December 24)

BIOGRAPHICAL DICTIONARY

Rudolfo Anaya (1937–), a writer born in Pastura, is best known for his book *Bless Me, Ultima*. He taught for many years at the University of New Mexico.

Elfego Baca (1865–1945) was a sheriff in Socorro County who became famous for a shoot-out with Texas outlaws. He later became a lawyer and politician.

Jimmy Santiago Baca See page 78.

William "Billy the Kid" Bonney See page 50.

Kit Carson See page 49.

Jeff Bezos (1964–), born in Albuquerque, had an interest in computers as a child. In high school, he started an educational summer camp for children. Bezos founded the online retailer Amazon.com in 1994 and bought the *Washington Post* newspaper in 2013.

Francisco Vásquez de Coronado (c. 1510–1544) was a Spanish explorer who led an expedition into New Mexico and the surrounding area in 1540.

Estevan "Estevenico" Dorantes (?–1539) was a former enslaved African who traveled with Marcos de Niza to New Mexico in 1539. Estevanico was the first outsider to encounter the Pueblo people. He was killed at Zuni Pueblo.

Tom Ford (1961–) is a fashion designer and film director. Ford was born in Texas but spent most of his childhood in Santa Fe. He started his own fashion brand in 2005.

Joe Garcia See page 89.

Geronimo (1829–1909) was a leader of the Chiricahua Apaches who was born in what is now western New Mexico. In the 1880s, he fought U.S. troops while trying to avoid being forced onto a reservation.

Robert Goddard See page 58.

R. C. Gorman (1931–2005) was a prominent Navajo artist, renowned for his colorful images of Native American women. Born in Arizona, he moved to Taos in 1968. There he opened the Navajo Gallery, the first art gallery owned by a Native American.

Geronimo

R. C. Gorman

Michelle Lujan Grisham (1959–) was sworn in as a U.S. Representative for New Mexico in 2013. Born in Los Alamos and raised in Santa Fe, Grisham received undergraduate and law degrees from the University of New Mexico. When Grisham was the state's Department of Health secretary, she fought to ban the sale of junk food in schools.

Sid Gutierrez (1951–), an astronaut born in Albuquerque, was the first Latino to lead a space shuttle mission.

William Hanna (1910–2001) teamed up with Joseph Barbera to create cartoon characters such as Tom and Jerry and Scooby-Doo. Over his long career, Hanna won seven Academy Awards and eight Emmy Awards. He was born in Melrose.

Neil Patrick Harris (1973–), born in Albuquerque, is an actor, producer, singer, and director. He was the longtime star of the TV show *How I Met Your Mother*.

Tony Hillerman (1925– 2008) wrote popular mystery novels set on Navajo lands in New Mexico. He lived in Albuquerque.

Conrad Hilton See page 101.

Neil Patrick Harris

Allan Houser (1915–1994) was a Chiricahua Apache sculptor who studied and worked in Santa Fe. He is known for his graceful statues of Native Americans.

Minka Kelly (1980–) is a television and film actress. She was born in Los Angeles, California, and raised in Albuquerque.

Jean Baptiste Lamy (1814–1888) was a Roman Catholic priest who built many churches and schools in New Mexico.

Octaviano Larrazolo See page 86.

George López See page 75.

Nancy Lopez See page 79.

Demi Lovato (1992–) got her start as an actress and singer on the TV show *Barney & Friends* when she was seven years old. She was born in Albuquerque.

Mabel Dodge Luhan (1879–1962) was a wealthy world traveler who settled in Taos. She invited painter Georgia O'Keeffe, photographer Ansel Adams, and other artists and writers to stay at her home, helping make Taos a center for the arts.

Tony Hillerman

Maria Martinez

Georgia O'Keeffe

Antonio José Martínez (1793–1867) was a Native American priest who championed the rights of the Pueblo. He set up the first school in Taos and had the first printing press in New Mexico.

Esther Martinez (1912–2006) was a storyteller who drew on her Native American culture. She was a native of the Ohkay Owingeh (San Juan) Pueblo.

Maria Martinez See page 74.

Susana Martinez See page 85.

Colt McCoy (1986–), born in Hobbs, plays professional football. At the University of Texas, McCoy became the winningest quarterback in college football history, with 45 victories.

George McJunkin See page 25.

N. Scott Momaday See page 70.

Roy Nakayama See page 96.

Janet Napolitano (1957–) served as governor of Arizona and secretary of the U.S. Department of Homeland Security. In 2013, Napolitano became president of the University of California. She was raised in Albuquerque.

Marcos de Niza (c. 1495–1558) was an Italian friar who, in 1539, led the first European expedition into New Mexico. He claimed to have found one of the Seven Cities of Cíbola during the trip, prompting further exploration of the region.

Georgia O'Keeffe See page 76.

Juan de Oñate (c. 1550–1626) was a wealthy merchant in New Spain who led the first band of European settlers into New Mexico. As governor of New Mexico, he treated the Pueblo people brutally and was later tried for his cruel actions.

Janet Napolitano

Katherine Ortega

J. Robert Oppenheimer (1904–1967) was a scientist who ran the Manhattan Project at Los Alamos. He and his team of 3,000 people developed the first atomic bomb.

Katherine Ortega (1934–) served as the U.S. treasurer from 1983 to 1989. She is a native of Tularosa.

Alfonso Ortiz See page 30.

Adelina Otero-Warren See page 57.

Popé (?–1692) was a San Juan Pueblo priest who wanted to preserve Pueblo life. He and other priests urged the Pueblo to resist Spanish culture and religion. In 1680, they led the Pueblo Revolt, which drove the Spaniards from the region.

Ernie Pyle (1900–1945) was a journalist who lived for a time in Albuquerque. He wrote about U.S. soldiers during World War II and was killed during combat in the Pacific.

Bill Richardson (1947–) served as governor of New Mexico from 2003 to 2011. The son of a Mexican mother and a white father, he became interested in politics during college. After settling in Santa Fe in 1978, Richardson was elected to the U.S. House of Representatives. He also served as U.S. ambassador to the United Nations.

Millie Santillanes (1932–2007) was a city clerk, small business owner, and community activist in Albuquerque. She founded the New Mexican Hispanic Culture Preservation League in 1998.

Leslie Marmon Silko (1948–) was born in Albuquerque and grew up on the Laguna Pueblo reservation in New Mexico. An award-winning novelist and poet, Silko also writes essays about the Native American experience.

Jarrin Solomon (1986–), a native of Albuquerque, is a sprinter won a bronze medal at the 2012 London Olympics in the 4 x 400-meter relay event. Solomon competed for Trinidad and Tobago, his father's home country.

Luci Tapahonso (1953–) is a Navajo poet from Shiprock. She was raised in a household where little English was spoken. To this day, she writes her poetry in the Navajo language and then translates it into English.

Luci Tapahonso

J. Paul Taylor

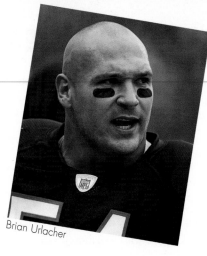

Brian Urlacher

J. Paul Taylor See page 108.

Miguel Trujillo See page 62.

Al Unser (1939–) is part of an Albuquerque family famous for producing top race-car drivers. He is one of only three people to win the Indianapolis 500 four times. His son **Al Unser Jr. (1962–)** has won the Indianapolis 500 twice.

Brian Urlacher (1978–) is one of the top linebackers in the National Football League. Born in Washington State, he moved to Lovington, New Mexico, as a child and later became a top college player at the University of New Mexico.

Don Diego de Vargas (?–1704) was a Spanish soldier who led the reconquest of New Mexico in 1692, after the Pueblos had driven Spanish settlers from the colony.

Susan Wallace See page 52.

Annie Dodge Wauneka See page 63.

Jim White See page 16.

Cathay Williams (1842–1924) was born into slavery in Missouri. During the Civil War, she disguised herself as a man and served as a soldier. She later was sent to New Mexico and was part of the Buffalo Soldiers.

Cheryl Willman See page 100.

Al Unser Jr.

RESOURCES

★ ★ ★

BOOKS

Nonfiction

Cunningham, Kevin, and Peter Benoit. *The Pueblo*. New York: Children's Press, 2011.

Friedman, Mark. *The Apache*. New York: Children's Press, 2011.

Green, Carl R., and William R. Sanford. *Billy the Kid*. Berkeley Heights, N.J.: Enslow Publishers, 2009.

Green, Carl R., and William R. Sanford. *Kit Carson: Courageous Mountain Man*. Berkeley Heights, N.J.: Enslow Publishers, 2013.

Rubin, Susan Goldman. *Wideness and Wonder: The Life and Art of Georgia O'Keeffe*. San Francisco: Chronicle Books, 2010.

Thompson, Linda. *Traveling the Santa Fe Trail*. Vero Beach, Fla.: Rourke Educational Media, 2013.

Weigle, Marta, Frances Levine, and Louise Stiver. *Telling New Mexico: A New History*. Santa Fe, NM: Museum of New Mexico Press, 2009.

Fiction

Abraham, Susan Gonzales. *Cecilia's Year*. El Paso, Tex.: Cinco Puntos Press, 2004.

Anaya, Rudolfo. *Bless Me, Ultima*. New York: Warner Books, 1994.

Anaya, Rudolfo. *Serafina's Stories*. Albuquerque: University of New Mexico Press, 2004.

Little, Kimberley Griffiths. *The Last Snake Runner*. New York: Dell Laurel-Leaf, 2004.

Taschek, Karen. *Horse of Seven Moons*. Albuquerque: University of New Mexico Press, 2004.

Visit this Scholastic Web site for more information on New Mexico:
www.factsfornow.scholastic.com
Enter the keywords **New Mexico**

AUTHOR'S TIPS AND SOURCE NOTES

★ ★ ★

Ever since I first learned about the Taos Pueblo, I've been fascinated with the people and places of New Mexico. Since 1996, I've taken three trips there. The most recent one was in 2006, to do research for this book.

A number of books and Web sites helped expand my knowledge of New Mexico's history and culture. To learn more about the Pueblos, Navajos, and Apaches, as well as the Ancestral Pueblos who came before them, I consulted Raymond Friday Locke's *The Book of the Navajo* and David E. Stuart's *Anasazi America*. Also helpful were Alvin M. Josephy's *500 Nations* and the various nations' and pueblos' Web sites.

For general New Mexico history, I read several books by Marc Simmons of the University of New Mexico. The most helpful was *New Mexico: An Interpretative History*. For more recent events, I relied on *New Mexico: Past and Future*, by Thomas E. Chávez, and *Larger Than Life: New Mexico in the Twentieth Century*, by Ferenc M. Szasz. A useful book for learning more about sites I haven't visited yet was Nancy Harbert's *New Mexico*. Online editions of two of the state's major newspapers, the *Albuquerque Journal* and the *Santa Fe New Mexican*, kept me informed on the latest news.